Blythington's Game

Featuring

Taylor Smart

Blythington's Game

King's Way Press
3721 New Macland Rd.
Suite 200-141
Powder Springs, GA 30157
www.kwp-books.com

Blythington's Game

The Raventon Mysteries

featuring Taylor Smart

for our daughter, **Kristyn Mikayla Watters**

The most magical, optimistic, and irreplaceable moments on one's timeline of life are those moments of precious innocence, no matter how short or long those moments might last, moments when nothing seems beyond grasp, when everything is a brass ring, when life itself is the raw material out of which dreams are forged, when the heavens hang within easy reach, when energy flows the fastest, when creative and intellectual inspirations are constant companions, when impossibilities are possible regardless of who say otherwise, when deferred gratification and sacrifice are prices worth paying, and when the fruits of tireless effort are the sweetest, long before the weight of experiences taints our outlook with cynicism and insists on imposing on our dreams the unshakable will of boundaries and barriers.

I long for those moments once again, personally, but I also see the awareness of such moments rising in Kristyn, and I smile because I know there is ***nothing*** in this world she cannot do, nowhere she cannot go, no chasms she cannot bridge, no challenges she cannot conquer. What is even better still is that I know that ***she*** knows it, too. My and Chris's love for Kristyn is boundless, without barriers or conditions. And the world is a better place because of her.

Endeavor to persevere.

-- George Wootton

Persevere your endeavors.

-- *mark randolph watters*

Acknowledgment and Thanks

My eternal gratitude to Chris Watters and Kristyn Watters for their much-needed help in finding and eliminating that which eludes my discovery – incorrect punctuation; misspelled words; excess words; inconsistencies; and every other mistake known to haunt the pages of every writer. This may not be a great book, but it's far better after the benefit of your keen eyes.

I love you both more than this writer's words can express.

The Game Pieces

The Raventon Mysteries

Book 2

Blythington's Game

Featuring

Taylor Smart

Prologue

"You want ... *what* for your birthday?" Susan Smart asked Mike.

"You heard me," he replied, smiling.

"Men are all alike; consumed by gadgetry. Where's the romance?"

"I wouldn't put this in the gadgetry category. And, for your information, it's one big *hunk* of romance. You, of all people, should know that."

"Maybe, but ... *really?*"

"Really. I've got to go, or I'll miss my flight." Mike gave Susan a hug and kiss. "Bye, Taylor!"

"Bye, Dad!" Taylor shouted in return. "Bring me something!"

"Will do, Mewels. And mind you stay out of mischief! Summer's winding down and–"

"Dad," Taylor said, smiling, revealing her head around the corner at the top of the stairs, "aren't you mistaking me for Bobbie Leigh Harwell?"

Mike returned her smile with a wink. "No mistake here." He turned to Susan and whispered, "I received an email this morning from Uncle Joe's attorney."

"Josie? About what?"

"About his blasted Will."

"That thing *still* not probated?"

"Nope, but his attorney said some strange things, in choppy terms, things like 'expect the pieces to fall into place soon' and 'have had our people watching' and 'we now know how to proceed', spooky things like that."

"Did he say you're involved in any way? I mean, isn't his a rather large estate? Is this something that's going to require our services?"

"Didn't say. I have to presume that just my *getting* the email implies such. We'll see, I suppose. Oh, well, gotta go."

1

The Shop

Miss Peasy sat in one of the white wing-backed wicker chairs gracing the sprawl of her front porch. She took a draw on her cherrywood pipe, releasing its swirl of smoke into the summer air, waving as she did to Taylor and Susan, both of whom were off to explore downtown Raventon's historical treasures, namely its shops. No one could have predicted the smoldering ember of adventures awaiting Taylor within the depths of one of those shops.

"Flying today, Miss Peasy?" Taylor asked.

"There's too windy a draft aloft, I'm afraid, Taylor," she replied. "And storms on the horizon. Maybe tomorrow. Join me if you'd like."

"Anything we can get for you while we're in town?" Susan asked, more to redirect the subject.

Miss Peasy glanced around, looking for reminders. "Got my pipe tobacco. Got my licorice. Got my cider. Oh, yes! A couple of burgers would be nice, if you don't mind."

"Two Zippies, on their way!" Taylor shouted.

Miss Peasy took a long draw on her pipe and smiled.

The town offered much for its size. Nestled snug within the calming undulation of the Appalachian foothills, like a cut diamond in a gold ring, Raventon passed its days quietly, with the relative exception of the cave incident. Taylor and Bobbie Leigh spoke of it still, while on occasion enjoying a Miss Peasy apple pie and comparing arrowhead finds. The town had elected a sheriff to succeed the ignominious fall of Hagan. Other than that hiccup, Raventon carried on, offering to outsiders no hints as to its other festering issues.

Besides the recreation and scenery of Lake Jasper, Sagitaw Falls, and a certain cave, the town was filled with historic sites, scenic parks, and nostalgic venues. Tourists and locals strolled the shaded sidewalks of downtown, as free of cares as the bluebirds flitting from branch to branch among the flowering white cherry trees thriving in the nearly mile-long stretch of Main Street's median. As carefree as a touristy town can be, that is to say, given its circumstances.

Raventon's homeless and jobless trudged without aim, long stripped of their dignity, among the well-to-do, holding crudely scripted slices of cardboard polygons that screamed their plights in ways their choked and charred voices no longer could. They clustered on corners and cluttered these same sidewalks, cigarette butts and abandoned signage marking their presence, the black-markered, block-lettered words begging for the privilege of work, or, cutting to the chase, food.

Shoppers and shopper-wannabes peered through the tall windows of storefronts enticing them with silent, desperate pleas to enter, to partake, to prime the pump of a local economy mired deep in its corner of financial distress.

One storefront in particular caught Taylor's eye this Saturday afternoon as she and Susan explored the downtown streets of their new hometown. On a corner at the end of Main and First, near the river, stood a homely building. Its chipped, rust-colored brickwork begged repair. Windows of stained glass soared from sidewalk to ceiling and courted an accumulation of years of airborne particulate, rendering the surface with a substance of sticky, grey opaqueness, similar, Taylor believed, to the crud-like mixture of dust and hairspray coating her bathroom sink.

Susan and Taylor at first thought the building abandoned, as it was flanked by empty structures of equally unkempt appearance. "Closed" or "For Lease" signs clung posted to their doors, signs of the times during the midst of an economic recession of historic proportions. Other signs, such as 'Bank-Owned' or 'Short Sale', gave notice of foreclosure, of the end of a cycle of prosperity.

The Smarts were among the few prospering in Raventon. Thanks in primary part to his year-long adventure as the captive of the town's former Sheriff, not to mention his extraordinary skills as a carpenter—Miss Peasy-endorsed—Mike Smart managed to keep a small backlog of repair and renovation jobs, mostly among the wealthy residents living in older homes within the historic district of downtown Raventon. This kept the family's income flowing steadily, augmented by Susan's monthly submissions to the magazines Home Manicure and Southland Experience.

Despite Mike's sound argument to the contrary, Susan could not help but feel a measure of guilt for their current well-being. Still, knowing such a lifeway could end in a cruel flash, without notice, she set aside such feelings and worked hard to improve her skills as a writer and to broaden her scope of contacts and clients. Moreover, she carved out time daily to give thanks and to offer her services as a volunteer to the community.

Susan's attention turned to a block-lettered red 'OPEN' sign hanging by the tilt of imbalance on a bent doornail, like an abandoned ornament. Disinterested, perhaps bored, Taylor thought nothing of the eyesore and was drawn instead to the rhythmic clatter of a tourist-borne, horse-pulled carriage ambling with a rhythmic clackity-clack down the broad, cobblestoned street.

Filled with the sort of curiosity one might feel upon confronting an oversized, unopened gift box, Susan stopped. After chiseling dust and goo and opaqueness from a small area, she walled each side of her face with her palms to block out glare. She pressed her forehead against the window. She gasped. What she saw fascinated her.

"Taylor, let's take a look inside *this* store. What's its name?" she asked, searching right and left for a sign as she wiped her forehead clean of the window's grime.

"Right there, Mom," Taylor said, pointing to a timid rectangular sign hanging just above their heads, its raised lettering rusted and its paint as chipped as the brick it was anchored in.

"Unique Antiques. My kind of place! Let's take a look."

Taylor sighed. *What's the deal with old people and old things?* she thought.

The pair entered the store, releasing the tinkling sound of a tiny bell hanging above the door. They were met immediately with the scent of the ages, a smell that sent their senses hurtling a hundred years past, as if they had just walked through a time portal and into the clutch of their great-great-grandparents' armoire.

"*Brrr! Chilly* in here!" Susan noted wrapping herself in her arms.

"Well, it *is* the beginning of August, Mom."

"Nothing antique about the a/c in here."

Surrounding Susan and Taylor rested the tools, machines, toys, and implements of ages removed, items retired by progress to the shelter of history. Telephones; phonographs; furniture; weapons; trunks; clocks; radios; pocket watches; coins; chairs; books; sewing machines; lamps; tapestries; glassware; silverware; statuary. Each quiet object harbored tales trapped by time.

Susan wanted to surprise Mike with an antique radio, the floor-model kind, and perhaps she'd stumbled into the right place for such. She began her search, which took little more than a turn of her head.

Against the far wall was a row of radios, floor and table models, beautifully constructed units embellished with carved wood trim and the flowing curves of art deco. A floor model grabbed her attention, its shimmering carvings of maidenhair leaves marking its perimeter, polished as a crown jewel set amid crusted diamonds.

"*That's* the one!" she whispered as Taylor wondered off to other parts of the store. "I can practically *hear* it."

2

The Radio Challenge

Susan had an unspoken hope but no real expectation of an antique radio actually *working*, and, indeed, most of the radios in this shop failed the functional litmus test. This one did not fail. It worked well, *too* well, beyond *anyone's* imaginings.

Needing assistance, Susan peeked around the store for an employee. Seeing none, she stepped to the checkout counter, a refurbished mahogany bar polished to a mirror finish, complete with stools and flanked with oak cracker barrels filled with Maryjanes and wrapped miniature peanut butter logs. A sign against each barrel read, 'Take one, take two, but take three, and you're through!' The cash register's brass gleamed like gold. She tapped twice on the counter bell, which emitted a delightfully clear ring.

"Yes, ma'am, so sorry!" called the shop's owner as he scampered from the darkened recesses of the shop, wiping his hands in a white cloth. "Been repairing some clocks and didn't hear you come in. How may I help you?"

"*Love* this cash register!" Susan exclaimed, caressing its top as her eyes scanned the store. "Love your shop."

"Thank you. Beauty, ain't it? It's a National 332, a hundred and eight years old. Works like a charm."

"Nickel plate?"

"Nothing but; intact, too."

"You use this puppy to ring up sales?"

"If it costs ten dollars or less, yes," the owner said with a shrug. "Makes for a good show, and the kids love it. Truth be told, ain't no more a kid than me. Otherwise, it's the Dell and point-of-sale software. Not nearly as personal, this techie stuff, so I break out the 332 as often as possible."

"It's gorgeous. I wanted to ask about a radio, one of the floor models you have over there."

The shop owner gave a swift wipe to where Susan had touched the National 332 as she walked toward the row of radios. "Yes, ma'am, let's go take a look."

"It's this one," Susan said, pointing to the radio.

"Ah, yes, the Stromberg-Carlson. Best radio ever made, if you want my opinion. Still works, too."

"Still works?"

"Bottom-left knob," the owner directed.

Susan turned the knob, which replied with a comforting click.

"Let 'er warm up. Original tubes, you know."

"Original? Cool!"

"I take in only those antiques truest to their original condition."

After a couple of minutes, the long-forgotten, yet familiar buzz of frequency static and hum rose from the workings. Susan believed for a moment she might hear a Roosevelt fireside chat.

"Go ahead, find a station. AM, of course."

"Of course!"

Susan tuned the radio to AM 1540. The sound, while constrained by the technology of a former day, came through cracklingly clear.

Susan swept her palm across the radio's top and sides. Aside from an occasional scratch, none that indicated abuse, the surface was as flawless as the sound was reminiscent.

"How much?" Susan asked, smiling.

"Oh, it ain't for sale, ma'am," the owner replied.

"Ain't for sale?" Susan echoed with surprise. "You *are* an antiques dealer, aren't you?"

"Well, yes, but you see, ma'am, this is a very *special* radio. It's been ... in the family for a long time, and well, it's ... special."

"Even 'special' has its price. I'll give you a thousand dollars for it."

The owner sighed, his gaze fixed upon the Stromberg. He tilted his head. "I don't know–"

"Fifteen hundred?" Susan pressed.

After a long pause, Susan blurted, "Two thousand dollars. I must *have* this radio!"

"*Three* thousand, plus tax," the owner replied.

"Whoa. Indeed 'special' *does* have a price after all, and a *steep* one at that!"

The owner laughed. "Didn't expect that sort of price to ever be accepted, ma'am. Still don't, but it *does* sort of ease the pain of letting go."

"I'll *bet* it does." Susan gazed at the owner and then at the radio. "Well, I haven't *accepted* it yet. Okay, maybe I *have* accepted your price. It's too gorgeous to pass up, but *three thousand dollars?* This Stromberg over here is only $300."

"But it don't work, ma'am. Missing most of its guts. See?" The shop owner slid the Stromberg forty-five degrees. "This here Strommy is *special*, believe me."

Susan glanced around the store, looking for Taylor, and after a moment's thought, replied, "Is it special just because it *works?* I mean, it's not like it'll play the old radio shows. But, if *that's* your price, then ... Okay, *done!* I'll take it. But you have to *deliver* it."

"Cost you an extra hundred," the owner answered sternly. "Just *kidding*, ma'am! If you live within a twenty-mile radius, we deliver free."

"I should *hope* so! We live just up that hill, a couple of blocks away."

"It can be delivered this afternoon. Cash or charge?"

"Cash on the barrel head. I don't believe in credit, not anymore," Susan replied with a smile, peeling off hundred dollar bills.

"Good for you!" the owner agreed, staring in amazement at the roll of bills in Susan's hand. "Don't get many *cash-paying* customers anymore. Don't get many customers, *period*, anymore, what with the economy like it is. You ought not be carrying that much cash around here, ma'am."

"Downtown doesn't strike me as much of a crime risk, not in broad daylight," Susan replied, handing the owner thirty-three hundred-dollar notes. "Am I wrong?"

"You're not wrong, I reckon. But one can't be too careful, is all. One more thing, ma'am, speaking of crime risks."

"And that would be?"

"How would you rate *your* honesty, *your* integrity, on a scale of, say, one to ten?"

"What? Are you serious? You have my cash in your hand."

"*Very* serious, ma'am. It's vital I get your answer."

"Vital? In what regard?"

"Can't exactly say, ma'am."

"*Can't* say or *won't* say?"

"Just is. So, from one to ten–"

"Vital to the sale of this radio?" Susan interrupted, her frustration rising.

"Indeed. The new owner of this radio must meet the highest ethical standards."

"*Ethical* standards? I thought cash was the only required 'standard'."

"I really must have your answer, ma'am, or I will be forced to return your money."

Stunned at the owner's personal persistence, Susan took a step back, eyes widened and mouth open. Confronting such disrespect with any other transaction, Susan would have grabbed her cash and never returned. But, this was the radio.

"A *ten*, of course, if you must know. No, make that a *hundred!*"

"We shall see."

"You shall see *what?*"

"I'll be back in a moment, ma'am," the owner said, taking Susan's payment to retrieve her change.

Abruptly, the owner whisked away around the corner of the checkout area, through a beaded curtain. Susan waited, her wad of remaining cash dangerously exposed.

After several anxious minutes in which Susan heard nothing from behind the beaded curtain, she turned her attention to Taylor. As she moved toward Taylor, scanning an array of wall clocks, she noticed a squarish object on the floor, next to an old trunk.

"What's this?"

She reached to pick up the object, an engraved silver clip, its vise holding firm a thick fold of bills, the outer of which was a $100 note. Susan pulled the paper from the clip and counted. Four thousand dollars, all hundreds, more than enough to pay for the radio.

"What do you have, Mom?" Taylor asked.

"This," Susan replied, opening her hand and revealing the cash and silver clip.

Taylor gasped, swallowing her chewing gum.

"Four thousand dollars, Taylor."

"Mom, look at these bills," Taylor said, thumbing through the stack, "the dates and serial numbers. Looks like each one's a series-1966 red-sealed United States note!"

"And that's a good thing?"

"It's a *great* thing! A *rare* thing! These are in super shape, probably worth *twice* their face value. Dad has a few of these in his collection."

"I'm turning them in to the store owner."

"T–turning them *in?* Mom, he'll just pocket the cash, or worse, sell it as antique currency."

"Maybe. But this money isn't ours, Taylor."

Taylor looked into Susan's eyes. "You're right, of course. We have to turn in this money, but why not take it to the police?"

"Because it probably belongs to the store owner. Why else would it *be* here, on this floor? It is special currency, after all, perfect for an antique store."

As Susan spoke, the store owner returned from behind the beaded curtain.

"Ah, *there* you are," Susan said. "I have something for you." She handed the clip and cash to the store owner. "Four thousand dollars."

The shop owner took the clip of cash. "Indeed, you *are* an honest person. You could have kept this money. As you've probably noticed, there are no security cameras in my store. Can't afford them. Thank you, Mrs. Smart. For the money."

"Why do you care about my ethical standards?"

"Not so much that *I* care, ma'am. The original owner of your radio cares. He requested that the purchaser of this radio adhere to strict ethical standards. And you've done that. The clip of money was the surest way to test you, without your knowing you were being tested. You've passed his challenge."

"His *challenge?*"

The owner smiled, wiping his hands with a handkerchief pulled from his back pocket. Susan noticed the ornate swirl of three embroidered letters, 'B', 'J', and something.

Susan sighed. "As my daughter would say–'whatever!'"

Susan looked around the store as the owner counted her ninety dollars' change into her palm. "Something about your store, sir," she observed. "We'll definitely be back."

"Expect your radio around three o'clock, ma'am. And thanks!"

"Thank *you*, sir! You've given my husband another reason to smile ... unless, of course, he kills me first for spending three thousand dollars. But, hey, it's *my* money, fairly earned, and I'll do with it as I please," Susan declared, a chuckle tumbling forth. "Taylor? I'm done here. Ready?"

"And *how*! This place creeps me out."

"You should be used to dark, dank places by now."

"What I'd *prefer* getting used to is a nice sidewalk café and maybe a carriage ride through town."

"Hmmm. Sounds nice. Let's do it!"

"See you at three, ma'am."

"We'll be there! Thank you!"

"No," the owner corrected with a whisper. "Thank *you*!"

3

The Envelope

"Careful," Susan said as she guided the men's steps through tricky ninety-degree turns and rooms filled with antique furniture here and with stacks of still-unpacked boxes there. "Place it by the fireplace, please, against the wall."

"Mom, wouldn't it look better over here, next to the couch? The fireplace just makes it look so ... *old*," Taylor said.

"It *is* old!"

"I know it is, but why call attention to it?"

"That's precisely the *point*, Taylor. Antiques *want* attention called to their oldness. You don't like the radio?"

"It's okay, I guess ... in a *prehistoric* sort of way."

"It's *art*, Taylor! Just *look* at it! Tiger maple. Lattice carvings. Mahogany inlays. I bet Bobbie Leigh'll like it."

"Don't count on it."

"Just don't see this sort of thing anymore, sweetheart, not often, anyway." Susan brushed her fingertips lightly across its top. "I can practically *hear* Fibber McGee and Molly–"

"*Who* McGee *and what?* Like I said–*prehistoric!*"

"You'll get used to it. You have to agree it *is* a beautiful piece of furniture!"

"I suppose." Taylor tilted her head side to side, exploring different perspectives. "Does it work?"

"It did in the shop. Let's give it a try."

Susan turned the on-off knob gently clockwise, forcing a mellow click.

Nothing.

She turned the volume knob.

Nothing.

"Mom!" Taylor said, pointing floorward.

"What!"

"Might help to plug it in."

Susan looked. "Oh, yeah. That *would* help."

"You think?"

"Don't get *smart*, Smart!" Susan smiled as she reached to insert the two-pronged connection to the early twenty-first century.

Making that minor, yet significant, adjustment, Susan tried again. The radio hummed, sounding a bit like Dr. Frankenstein's laboratory. She turned the frequency knob to AM 1540.

"Ah, loud and clear!" Susan declared amid the frequency's crackling. "Well, maybe not so *clear*."

"But definitely *loud*," chimed Taylor.

"Excuse me, ma'am. Sign here, please," one of the delivery men said.

"Certainly. On this line?"

"Yes, ma'am."

Susan took the clipboard, signed the delivery receipt and handed it, along with a fifty-dollar tip, back to the man, who returned a copy of the receipt to Susan.

"Congratulations, ma'am. Much obliged," the man said with a wink as he inserted the bill into his pocket. "And ... good luck."

Susan smiled, thinking the man's last remark a bit odd but dismissed it as a gesture of common courtesy extended to all customers of Unique Antiques.

"Will I *need* it?" Susan replied with an uneasy chuckle, referring to luck.

"Sound *is* a tad scratchy," said the man. "Luck? Time will tell. Probably a wise investment, though. Might want to cool this place down a bit," the man observed, removing his cap and wiping sweat from his forehead. "And I ain't sure the *fireplace* is the *best* place for an antique of this caliber. Might want to reconsider."

The men turned and exited, before Susan could give words to her reply.

"*Probably* a wise investment? Cool this place down? It's already like a fridge in here! Oh, well. Whatever."

"Mom, what was *that* all about?"

"You thought it strange, too?"

"Yes, sort of. Did you see him sweating? Probably because of that thick, black hoodie he was wearing. Could hardly see his face."

"That *was* odd, now that you mention it. He kept his head tilted down, too. It's ... it's sixty-eight degrees in here," Susan noted, craning her neck to read the thermostat.

"Was the radio *that* heavy?"

"To break a sweat? Don't think so," Susan said, tilting the radio forward. "Nope. Not heavy at all. Just hot-natured was he, I suppose."

"What did he mean by 'good luck'?"

Susan turned up the volume. "Who knows? Hey, sounds pretty good after a time to warm up, don't you think?"

"In a *prehistoric* sort of way, yeah. Do you mind if I look inside it, check out the tubes and junk? Listen to it a while, maybe?"

"Okay, I guess, but handle with care. In fact, don't handle the internals at all; just look. Those tubes are original and very hard—not to mention expensive—to replace."

"Got it, Mom. Thanks."

Susan departed for the kitchen to pour a glass of sweet iced tea.

Taylor gave the on/off knob a clockwise click. The radio buzzed increasingly louder as it warmed up. Taylor turned the frequency knob in search of a station. Then, the radio went cold, silent. As Mike would do, Taylor tapped the radio's top, harder each time, hoping to somehow spank life back into it. Then it occurred to Taylor to check the plug; she found it lying lifeless on the floor.

"Hmm. I thought mom ..."

Re-plugging the radio, a station arose to static-filled life, the words of the announcer fading in and out. Taylor listened.

"WonVillingham's last will and ...," the announcer spoke, some words trailing off, "... lost somewhere in Raventon, between the sounds and sites so loved by its citizens ... his estate, worth hundreds of millions ... will was never probated ..."

Taylor clicked the knob counter-clockwise and slowly slid the radio ninety degrees, exposing its workings. She touched the warm tubes and coils. Her curiosity pushed lightly the small wires going this way and that. "Won ... what?"

Then it caught her eye. A yellowed corner of paper extended perhaps an inch from under the workings.

The original owner's manual? Taylor wondered. *This dinosaur comes with instructions!*

Taylor reached to give the document a gentle touch, afraid it might crumble to powder if she pulled it. Confirming its relative pliability, Taylor slowly tugged on the corner, soon revealing several more inches and noticing it wasn't a document at all, but rather an envelope, sealed with a reddish-burgundy-colored wax stamp, pressed with an Old-English-styled letter 'W'.

"What have we here?" came her whispered question.

Taylor carefully separated the seal from the paper, crumbs of dried wax falling to the floor. Slowly, she pulled out the tri-folded document within and, opening its folds, scanned the handwritten message, its ink in places blurred and smudged but legible still. She separated the several papers, opening her mouth to call for her mom. Thinking otherwise, Taylor decided to let this discovery be her own. Perhaps this was an antique within an antique, the rewards of which belonged to its finder. She read silently:

Dear you (yes, YOU!),

Congratulations on your acquisition of this fine radio, particularly on your discovery of this envelope. This radio belonged to me during my glory days, days now long passed. It can be a most exceptional investment for you. Owners before you have had this same radio, this same envelope within centimeters of their fingertips, if not nestled within the warmth of their very palms, yet they failed to exercise their curiosity enough to take the next crucial step.

Life for them carried on, and, for better of for worse, ordinariness dominating their existence, as if nothing changed. But you CAN take that next crucial step. So again, I congratulate you.

And I beware you, too for it is only fitting I should do this.

They say that curiosity killed the cat. On the contrary, should you choose to proceed with my Game, you just might realize the OPPOSITE of that trite cliché—that curiosity EMBOLDENED, ENLIVENED, even ENRICHED the cat.

But, don't misunderstand. There are risks.

Considerable risks.

Shall we say ... cat-killing risks.

But, the rewards of this game are immense, should you complete all the requirements.

ALL of the requirements. Not 90% of the requirements; not 95%; not even 99.99%. ALL%.

It is ESSENTIAL you follow each instruction to its letter and complete each task in its every detail. Failure to do so will result in ... well, let's focus on the positive—those immense rewards I spoke of—shall we?

But first, you have a major decision to make.

Right here.

Right now.

If you are game to accept my Game, then look on the bottom right corner of this radio. This will then be your first of many moments of truth.

You will find a small latch. Turning the latch will open a compartment. *But beware!* Once the seal of the latch is breached, there is NO turning back. You are committed to play the Game. You may be tempted to walk away—others have so done, to their detriment—but DO NOT. Did I mention cat-killing risks?

Remove the document within the compartment. This one-of-a-kind document of vellum has been rolled and tied with a RED SATIN RIBBON, a detail you will discover is significant to your ultimate success. If you lose the ribbon, you lose the Game. Do not lose the Game.

I cannot overstate that once opened, failure to proceed in full compliance with the instructions will result in ... well, there is no way to sugarcoat this—your painful death.

There, I said it. Don't ask how such death will befall you. You do NOT want to know. Just know of it. But, should you proceed, following to the letter each detail of each instruction of each challenge, when completed your rewards will eclipse any of your expectations and in ways that will utterly and positively alter your lives and the lives of many others, many of whom you will never know.

You may use all your tools of imagination to complete each instruction; there are multiple paths to *the correct results. But where the instructions are specific, FOLLOW them!*

So ... are you game?

I think you are. I have confidence that you are. Do YOU have confidence?

Decide now.

Either return this document to its envelope and replace it where you found it, as have many others before you, or unlatch the latch and let the Game begin. All decisions are final. Once the latch is opened and the vellum removed, you CANNOT change your mind.

Oh, and one last thing. You will confront—and be tested by—many of your WORST FEARS.

So, with that said, have fun!

BJW

1975

"O ... kay," Taylor uttered, disbelief guiding her fingers as they turned the document, as if expecting to find some corporate logo shouting 'Fooled Ya, Inc.'. "I think Bobbie Leigh might want to know about this."

"What's that, sweetie?" Susan shouted from the kitchen.

"Nothing, Mom. Nothing. Um ... just marveling at this old radio. Quite an antique!"

"Indeed it is. So you like it now? Not the dinosaur you thought it was?"

"Sure! What's not to like?"

"Want a sandwich?"

"Sandwich? Later, maybe. Going over to Bobbie Leigh's," Taylor said, replacing the vellum inside the red-wax-sealed envelope and tucking same under her shirt. "Back in a couple of hours."

"See you later, then. Have fun!"

"Will do. Later!"

"Oh, while you're going, can you drop off this pie pan to Miss Peasy for me?"

"Mom, she'll take me prisoner for an *hour*, longer even, going on and on about the cave and such."

"Just place it on her porch, then. I'll call her in a few minutes and let her know."

"Okay," Taylor agreed, taking the pie pan from Susan. "Thanks, Mom. Bye!"

4

The Decision

This is a game? Taylor thought as she swerved to avoid potholes and branches filling the road like an obstacle course. *Some game! More like a sick joke. Maybe Bobbie Leigh knows something about this 'BJW' person or whatever it is.*

Taylor skidded to a halt in front of Bobbie Leigh's home. Her focus on leaf-raking, Bobbie Leigh gave an annoyed glance in response to the unseen source of the noise.

"Mewels!" she shouted, recognizing the noisemaker. "You're going to ruin your tires doing that! Lend me a hand and grab a rake!"

"Then *you* must have a *whole garage-full* of ruined tires!" Taylor picked a rake from a group of three leaning against an oak and began to rake. “Got something you need to see, Bobbie Leigh.”

“As long as it’s not homework or a Justin Bieber poster, I’m game!”

Taylor sighed. “It’s neither, but it *will* require your attention. And some reading. And interesting you should mention the word 'game'.”

“*Sounds* like homework!” Bobbie Leigh said, shaking her head.

“Believe me, it *ain’t* homework. Not like we think of homework, anyway.”

“Okay, now you’re turning into a mystery, Tay. Spill it!”

Taylor reached under her sweatshirt and removed the envelope. “By the way, do you know who might belong to the initials BJW?”

“BJW? BJW ... hmmm,” Bobbie Leigh said, mulling the letters. “No, I can’t seem to ... hey, wait a sec. I *do* know those initials! BJW. None other than the infamous–and I do mean *infamous*–Blythington Jehosiphats WonVillingham.”

“Blything ... *who?* Never mind; tell me later. Check this out.”

Bobbie Leigh gazed curiously upon Taylor as she took the envelope. "Sealed with *wax? Red* wax?"

"More like a burgundy-red wax."

"What *is* this, an invitation to the Debutante Ball?"

"The *what* ball?"

"*Debutante* Ball," Bobbie Leigh repeated.

"Is that one of those new-fangled, double-stitched, kangaroo-hide baseballs?" Taylor asked.

Bobbie Leigh sighed and lifted what remained of the red-wax seal, pulling out the document. Seconds passed as she read, her eyes fishtailing to and fro, her eyebrows jumping a time or two, as if afflicted with a nervous twitch. She absorbed the penned words.

"Vellum," Bobbie Leigh said, as she finished reading. "Wow. So ... what's vellum?"

"Sort of like a new-fangled, double-stitched, kangaroo-hide Debutante Ball, only it's parchment," Taylor replied with a cocked grin, Bobbie Leigh's deer-in-the-headlights eyes bulging. "It's paper made from animal skin."

"What?"

"I know, it sounds yucky, but this stuff lasts *forever*. Supposed to be the finest material on which to write. Sort of makes this mystery worth pursuing, don't you think?"

"I—I don't know. Have you removed the vellum document?"

"Not yet. Wanted to run it by you first. Are you game? Want to do this with me? And who is this Blythington fellow anyway?"

"Blythington Jehosiphats WonVillingham."

"*Jehosiphats?* What sort of parents would name their kid *that?* I mean, Blythington's bad enough, but *Jehosiphats?*"

"This guy is *bad news*, Taylor!"

"What do you mean?"

"They say—that is, I've been *told*—that BJW, a born-and-raised lifetime resident of Raventon, made millions in the insurance business."

"What sort of insurance business?"

"All kinds, I reckon. Nobody's really sure, exactly; except that I know my grandparents once bought a life insurance policy from him, a policy for their business, too. A quarter of a million dollar life policy, I think it was. Have you and your mom been over to WonVillingham Park, across the river off Summit Drive?"

"No, not yet."

"It's a pretty nice park. Modern playgrounds and a new skateboard facility; baseball fields; sand and nets for volleyball; an amphitheater for musicians and mimes; and lots of shaded space to picnic and open space to hoist a kite. Hiking trails, too. Not too shabby for a town Raventon's size. Anyway, BJW donated the money and land to build and maintain it—an endowment they call it, whatever *that* is. He's given Raventon millions of dollars over the years, I'm told, but the strange thing about it is that, despite all his charity and such, he's been arrested and tried for no fewer than *six murders*—and acquitted for each and *every* one! My *grandparents* were two of those murders."

"Are you *kidding* me? Is this BJW still living?"

"Let's go get your bike. I want to show you something."

"Okay," Taylor agreed, "but now you've really got my curiosity up about the author of this ... this vellum."

"Mine, too. And yes, I'm game if you are. Sounds like one big practical joke, but I'll play along."

"Practical joke or no, we can't tell our parents. Not yet."

"Not *ever!*" Bobbie Leigh said. "Tell *my* parents? Mine wouldn't listen anyway, but on the off-chance they *did* listen, they'd probably send me to boarding school, just to put a lid on any active conversation concerning BJW."

"Let's go get my bike," Taylor said, dropping the rake.

Bobbie Leigh climbed aboard her bike and rode circles around a trotting Taylor.

"When you gonna get a new bike, Tay?"

"It's *Muley*, okay? M-u-l-e-y."

"I thought it was M-e-w-e-l-s."

"Well, yeah, that too, but *not* Tay."

"Okay, Muley. For your stubbornness with beating your cancer, right?"

"That's right. Been six years now. I used to keep a ribbon tied around my wrist, to remind me of my fight and to never give up."

"Cool. Now, about the bike ..."

"Maybe for my birthday. I want one of those Path-10 bikes. You know, the 27-speed mountain bikes—"

"Yeah, the ones that cost a couple grand and sit in your garage nine months out of the year!"

"*That* much?" Taylor asked, stopping her trot dead in the middle of the road, near her front yard and a few feet in front of Bobbie Leigh.

"*Look out!*" Bobbie Leigh shouted swerving at the last second.

"Sorry, BL! But *two thousand dollars? Really?*"

"Really. And that's for the *cheap* Path-10 models. A Huffy's just as good. Besides, who needs twenty-seven speeds? Five at the most, if that. I get by with three."

"To keep up with you, I need *twice* twenty-seven!"

"*BL?* Did you call me ... BL?

"Get used to it," Taylor replied, prying chunks of mud from her tennis shoe bottoms. "Two can play this game. My revenge, you know."

"I *hate* it. It's one letter short of a *sandwich!*""

Taylor chuckled. "C'mon, let me show you the radio."

"Yeah, *this* I gotta see," Bobbie Leigh said, dropping her bike to the ground as she dismounted.

The girls entered the house and were met in the foyer by Susan.

"Hi, Bobbie Leigh," Susan greeted, sipping a glass of tea.

"Hi, Mrs. S.," Bobbie Leigh said, nose in the air. "*Mmmm!* Smells like a recent Miss Peasy visit."

"What tipped you off?" Taylor asked with a wink.

"Indeed. She just dropped off another apple pie, fresh from her oven. She said this one had a couple of *secret* ingredients in it, guaranteed *better* tasting than her other pies."

"I hope her secret ingredient wasn't licorice spittle," Taylor said.

"Probably oregano, knowing her penchant for the unexpected," Susan replied.

"This I gotta see!" said Bobbie Leigh.

"Hey, I thought it was the *radio* you 'gotta see'."

"Let's see 'em *both*, pie first!"

"Be right back with the pie, girls," Susan said with a smile. "Milk with that?"

"Yes, Mom." Taylor looked at Bobbie Leigh, who nodded. "Both of us. Thanks!"

"So this is the world-famous radio," Bobbie Leigh observed, gently touching its polished top. "Got the envelope?"

"Under my shirt," Taylor replied.

"So, what do we do next?"

"Says to take the document from the latched compartment under the radio."

"*Under* the radio? Down *there?*"

"I guess so. Sure looks 'under' to me. Help me tilt it so I can check it out."

"What if your mom sees us. I bet she won't like us messing with her new antique." Bobbie Leigh smiled at her choice of words. "*New* antique. That sounds weird!"

"Oxymoronic is more like it," Taylor observed.

"Oxy ... *what?*"

"I guess we should wait until *after* she brings back the pie and milk," Taylor whispered. "I think she's working on an article deadline, so my guess is she won't stick around."

"Where's your dad?" Bobbie Leigh asked.

"In New York City."

"New York City?"

"Yep. Which is why she had the radio delivered today. She wants it here to surprise him when he gets home next week. It's his birthday."

"What's he doing in New York City?"

"Something to do with his year-long ordeal with Sheriff Hagan and the cave. I think some morning TV shows and maybe some radio shows are interviewing him. Mom says there may be a book deal in the making. I know he's been talking to a New York publisher."

"Good for Mr. S. He deserves something decent to come out of his lost year and for all the grief you and your mom went through."

"You went through the grief, too, BL."

"Quite an experience," Bobbie Leigh said, turning. "I think I hear your mom coming."

"Here you are, girls!"

"Man, that smells good," Bobbie Leigh said. "Thanks, Mrs. S.!"

"You bet. Enjoy."

"Thanks, Mom."

"If you need me, I'll be upstairs in my office putting the finishing touches on my articles."

"For Home Manicure, Mrs. S.?"

"That, and another magazine. Antiques Quarterly."

"*That* explains the radio, Tay," Bobbie Leigh whispered.

"Dad's birthday explains the radio, too," Taylor said, returning the whisper. "Okay, Mom, we'll be out and about."

"Be careful. And stay out of caves!" Susan said, retreating up the stairs to her office.

"Okay, BL, help me tilt the radio. Careful, now. If this thing falls, we are *burnt* toast."

"What's with the BL? I *hate* that!"

"I *know*. Every time I say it, I get hungry, and you get mad," Taylor said, giving Bobbie Leigh a now-you-know-how-it-feels smile.

"Okay, I'm tilting it forward. It's not ... *so* heavy."

"Slowly now," Taylor advised. "Don't want to become a statistic of one, the only known death-by-entrapment under an antique floor radio."

Taylor stooped to the floor, onto her side, and maneuvered her head to get the proper view of underneath. Spider webs sagged to her face. She blew them aside.

"Find the latchy thing?"

"It's just a *latch*, BL, and yes, here it is."

"Open it and get the document out. This radio's getting heavy!"

"Hang on. No turning back, BL!" The wind pushed branches against the eve of the house, producing a perfectly-timed drum roll. "Here goes."

Taylor turned the oval-shaped, ivory latch ninety degrees, releasing the inch-thick, maple door, which lowered forty-five degrees on two squeaky hinges. Taylor stopped and listened, expecting her mom to respond, even though Susan was two floors up and well out of range. A tightly rolled document, yellowed and crisp, slid into Taylor's palm, as if pushed out. Carefully, Taylor pulled the document the remainder of the way out.

"Well? Do you have it?"

"Got it! And man, is it *crinkly* and stiff, like a potato chip!"

"Don't *break* it!" Bobbie Leigh said in a loud whisper. "And don't *eat* it, being as my initials make you hungry! And hurry out from there! Can't hold the radio like this much longer!"

"Let me just ... replace the latch door. There, it's latched ... okay, you can untilt it."

"Thank goodness!" Bobbie Leigh whispered and sighed. "Didn't seem all that heavy at first, but turns out it *was*."

"Check this out, BL!"

Bobbie Leigh gave Taylor a frown of playful frustration.

"Wow, you're right about the potato chip. Careful, Tay," Bobbie Leigh said. "Looks a *thousand years old!*"

"Yeah. Like a Dead Sea scroll, maybe?" Taylor ran the tips of her fingers over the document, fearful any pressure might tip the delicate balance between the whole and the sum of its parts. She sighed. "Ready, Bobbie Leigh? Remember, we're in this hip-deep. Make that *neck-deep*. No turning back. Westward ho, as they say. Face the music–"

"Will you *stop* with the dramatics and *open* it?" Bobbie Leigh blurted. "This is just somebody's idea of a stupid prank, anyway."

"Right."

Taylor began to slowly unroll the vellum document, stopping abruptly with every noisy crack and crinkle, afraid it might disintegrate to powder. "Before we do this, why don't you show me what you were going to show me."

"Show you? Show you *what?*"

"I don't know; back at your house, you just said you wanted to show me something."

Bobbie Leigh paused. "Oh yeah, now I remember. Okay, but let's take the document with us. Here, I'll place it inside my backpack."

"Careful, BL," Taylor said, helping to slide the document inside the backpack.

"I'm gonna *smack* you with this thing if you don't stop with the BL."

"No can do. It'd just evaporate."

The girls took a long gaze at each other and then burst out laughing.

Susan looked up from her keyboard upon hearing the door slam, knowing that wherever the two friends were off to, adventure was sure to follow.

5

Blythington Jehosiphats WonVillingham

(a thorn by any other name)

Taylor Smart and Bobbie Leigh Harwell leaned their bodies and bikes sharply into another of several ninety-degree-ish turns, blowing through stop signs and around parked cars and piles of curbside leaves, scattering panicked squirrels with the reckless abandon of thirteen-year-olds zeroed in on a mission, as they coursed the blur of their trek through oak-shaded downtown neighborhoods.

Elders sweeping Antebellum porches or watering baskets of hanging begonias lifted their heads just in time to witness the whoosh of the girls and their speeding bikes and to hear their laughter and intermittent shouts of questions and answers disappear with decreasing volume around the next bend. Shaking their white-crowned heads, wrinkled faces adorned with acknowledging smiles or approval, these elders resumed their chores, recalling the swirl and fragrance of their own youth-fueled adventures, priceless memories of carefree childhood days unencumbered by the smack of reality. Like welcomed pockets of cool air that meander unseen in the middle of a sweltering summer, these elders knew simply that Taylor Smart and Bobbie Leigh Harwell fulfilled the latest iterations of those cherished memories.

Blythington Jehosiphats WonVillingham, known conversationally among locals, if not dismissively, as Josie, was young once, so people said. Just when, and for how long, became questions asked and re-asked, the answers changing from telling to telling. Born in Raventon, supposedly in 1920, Blythington was the son of English parents who immigrated to America in 1919, in the aftermath of World War I. Blythington's father had served as a pilot in the Royal Flying Corps during that war.

Locals told embellished tales of how Josie acquired his legendary wealth, some insisting he never worked a day in his life, taking his millions in an inheritance. Others spoke of his wealth earned incrementally through a series of inventions, none of which amounted to much in terms of their time-tested usefulness or sustained popularity. Still, some spoke of his daring ways, how he headed up commercial river expeditions for the well-to-do to such remote places as the Amazon and on back-country survival trips through the Canadian Rockies, even taking well-paying groups to experience the midnight sun of the Arctic Circle. Such tales had long since occupied the realm of legend and lore, as Blythington Jehosiphats WonVillingham had not presented a public face in well over three decades. No one knew with any certainty that he had passed through the gates of eternity, despite the rumor of such as suggested by his headstone on Crepe Myrtle Hill.

"We have to bike up *that?*" Taylor asked between breaths, elbows propped on her handlebars, as the girls rested at the foot of the challenging slope.

Crepe Myrtle Hill loomed before them like a great castle wall, its headstones, monuments and mausoleums marking the mossed resting places of Raventon's regal.

"Afraid so, Tay. Or we can walk. Let's catch our breaths first."

"So, what were you going to show me is in the cemetery?"

"Indeed, this *very* cemetery."

"Glad it's the middle of the day!" Taylor observed, looking at the cotton-cloud sky. "Don't much care for cemeteries and darkness."

"I thought that living in that haunted house of yours would have given you opportunity by now to put spooks and junk behind you," Bobbie Leigh said, smiling.

"Spooks are *not* the sort of thing one easily puts behind," Taylor answered, gazing upon plot after plot of weather-worn headstone slabs pushed to a tilt by age and watched over by gnarled oak limbs and pocked, pointed obelisks, "especially if one is facing a whole *hill-full* of 'em."

"Truth spoken, girl."

"Anyway, what's a cemetery got to do with the BJW document?"

"You'll see. C'mon," Bobbie Leigh said, pulling Taylor with a wave of her arm.

"You're biking it?"

"Tougher to walk it. C'mon!"

Taylor issued a groan as she pushed her bike's pedals into the steep climb up Crepe Myrtle Hill. "Says *you!*"

"Over here, Muley!" shouted Bobbie Leigh.

Taylor pushed her pedals with a burst of energy, determined not to be outdone by Bobbie Leigh Harwell, climbing a couple hundred feet. She swung her right leg over the frame of her bike, dropping it as she did, the rattle of the metal echoing through the trees, and walked toward Bobbie Leigh.

"Sister, I have *got* to get me some legs like *yours!*" Taylor conceded, massaging her calves and sucking air.

"Look," Bobbie Leigh said.

Taylor followed the point of Bobbie Leigh's finger. She read. "'Blythington Jehosiphats WonVillingham. Born January 17, 1920. Lived hard. Worked hard. Played hard. Die hard.' He's *dead?*"

"Don't know."

"What do you mean you don't *know*? Here's his grave."

"All folks know for *sure* is that this is his *headstone*. Whether or not his cold bones're *underneath*, well, that's a matter for speculation," Bobbie Leigh replied.

Taylor studied the stone further.

"You know, now that you mention it, there's no death date on the slab."

Bobbie Leigh grinned, as Taylor realized this and other inconsistencies of the alleged grave. "That, and look at the words."

"They—they're all *past tense*. Except *'Die'*!"

"Precisely."

"So, if he's *not* dead, then ... where *is* he?"

"Question of the century, Tay. Ain't saying he's *not* dead, but nobody's seen hide nor hair of him in thirty years, and nobody's mentioned his name since he was found *not guilty* for killing my grandparents."

"*What?* This person *killed* your grandparents?" Taylor stared at the headstone. "How ... how did your grandparents die, Bobbie Leigh?"

"Stabbed while asleep in their beds, in the middle of the night. Police said it was a home invasion. Place was ransacked, stuff taken. I never knew my grandparents, of course, but I'm told they owed WonVillingham money, several months' rent for the house they lived in, as well as money they borrowed from him."

"Borrowed?"

"WonVillingham owned a business that made loans, sort of like one of those title-pawn stores that loan money against the title of your car."

"How much?"

"Too much. Several thousand, I'm told. More'n they could pay back. WonVillingham would have repossessed his own mother's car if she'd been late on any payment. As for the house they rented from him, they refused to pay him, saying he never maintained the place. Roof leaked; pipes leaked; needed painting; better insulation; appliances didn't work; things like that. Police found the supposed murder weapon at the scene with the initials 'BJW' on the knife's ivory handle. Everybody knew it belonged to

WonVillingham. He was the only one in town with ivory-handled knives and the initials BJW."

"So, how'd they find him innocent?"

"Not *innocent!* Just not guilty."

"Okay, not guilty. *Supposed* murder weapon?"

"Turns out the knife *wasn't* the murder weapon. Blood everywhere; the fatal injuries came from the strikes of a blunt object, like a hammer, but not a sharp instrument. No blood other than my grandparents'. WonVillingham even had a soundproof alibi."

"You mean *fool*proof ..."

"That, too. Nobody in the neighborhood heard *anything* and thus saw nothing. WonVillingham had reported a set of personalized ivory-handled knives, given to him by some African country's head of State, stolen in a burglary two years earlier. Detectives who visited WonVillingham that morning noted that his car's engine was cold, and he lived too far away to walk to my grandparents' house."

"Maybe he took a cab, or a friend drove him," Taylor speculated.

"They checked that out. Nothing. He had motive, all right, and the circumstances of the knife were awfully suspicious. Like I said, not guilty. Reasonable doubt, I reckon."

"Reasonable doubt?"

"Reasonable doubt. No direct evidence linking him to the crime, just like all the other murders this man was suspected of committing. So he walked. Again."

"Other murders?"

"Several others. In every case, evidence was either insufficient or witnesses refused to testify."

"Wow, what a bummer! I'm so sorry for your loss, Bobbie Leigh. You've been carrying this around for a long time. Are the police still looking for the killer?"

"Don't think so, 'cause everyone knows Josie's got to have been the killer. Just can't prove it, is all. Haven't heard anything more about it. The case is pretty chilly."

"Chilly? You mean cold?"

"Chilly, cold, whatever. Nothing more has come of it."

"That's too bad."

Bobbie Leigh and Taylor looked silently upon the mysterious BJW headstone.

"Let's assume he's dead and buried, right here, and get on with this," Taylor said, adding, "Speaking of 'chilly', this *place* gives me the chillys!"

Bobbie Leigh reached inside her back pack, retrieving the vellum scroll.

"Reckon who *is* buried here, Bobbie Leigh?"

"Maybe nobody."

"Then maybe BJW is watching us this very moment," Taylor noted, turning toward several of the huge oaks occupying the grounds. "If this *is* a prank, as you say, maybe he's got binoculars trained on us as we speak, laughing his ninety-five-year-old head off at his ... latest victims."

"You worry too much, Tay."

"Not really. Just wondering. So, untie the ribbon, and let's get to it."

Bobbie Leigh, despite her insistence the BJW scroll was nothing more than a prank, cleared her throat and looked into Taylor's eyes, hoping to discern some hint of a reason to go home, put the document back where they found it, and forget any of this happened. Taylor's eyes spoke nothing of the sort.

"Well? *Untie* it!" Taylor said.

"I ... uh ... what I mean is ..."

"Here, I'll do it." Taylor grabbed the document from Bobbie Leigh's quivering fingers.

"Careful!"

"Look, if this thing's real, we've passed the point of no return, so we might as well see what we're up against. If it's a hoax, let's get in on the laugh."

Taylor gripped one end of the satin red ribbon and pulled. The ribbon glided off the vellum into Taylor's hand. Taylor dropped the ribbon to the damp grass.

"No, Taylor!"

"What?"

"The *ribbon!* We need to *keep* the ribbon, remember?"

"Oh, yeah," Taylor said, plucking the ribbon. She draped it over Blythington's headstone. "Well ... here goes."

Taylor slowly unrolled the document.

"Lay it on the ground, Taylor, so you can flatten it out."

The girls knelt, placing the document atop low-cut grass. Slowly unrolling it to its unsettling sounds of crinkles, their eyes met with these unfurling loud words, in bold, Old-English-style calligraphy:

The Challenges

A Game of Life (and Death)

"Ha, ha! And *death,*" Bobbie Leigh muttered uncomfortably. "What a *hoot!*"

"Stop it, Bobbie Leigh. Let me read the first challenge."

"Looks like the *Constitution*, or something just as old," Bobbie Leigh observed, "all that fancy writing and looping letters and junk. Hey, what's that ... *sniff, sniff* ... smell?"

"Smell? I don't ... *sniff* ... smell anything."

"Suffering cemeteries!" came a voice approaching behind the girls. "What're you two up to?"

"Who said–?" Bobbie Leigh asked, turning. "Oh, it's *you* ... *sniff* ... Shoulda known."

6

Pilfree Romulus Bojo

(and the 'Good Death')

"Yep, it's me. Pilfree Romulus Bojo, in the flesh and at your service!"

"At your service?" Bobbie Leigh repeated, arms folded across her chest. "Who wants *your* service!"

"What's a Pil ...," Taylor asked, eyes fixed on the document. "What'd you say your name is? Pilfree ...?"

"Romulus Bojo. Like I *said*, in the flesh."

Taylor recognized the voice but not as that belonging to one Pilfree Romulus Bojo. She turned and stood.

"Hey, you're that brainy kid in eighth-grade," Taylor said, snapping her fingers, trying to place the face with a name.

Pilfree sighed. "Rubie," he said.

"Oh, *yeah. Rubie!*" Taylor remembered. "Cause you can knock out a Rubik's Cube in like ten seconds, or some ridiculous time. You've got quite the reputation ... Pilfree."

"As do you, Taylor Smart, what with the cave adventure and your missing dad. How's he doing?"

"Right as rain, he is. Got more carpentry jobs than he knows what to do with."

"Glad to hear it. Anyway, the reputation thing, that's just me bein' me, Rubik's Cubes and all. Rubie's my school name. Pilfree's my weekend name."

"*Weekend* name? Oh, brother," Bobbie Leigh said, her disgust accented by the gust of her sigh and an acute awareness of the ways of Pilfree. "In the *stinky* flesh, I might add. Pilfree Romulus Bojo, don't you *ever* bathe?"

"It's *summer*time, Bobbie Leigh Harwell, and ... well ... sweat *happens!*" Pilfree answered pridefully, giving his armpits a quick sniff, lest Bobbie Leigh be right. "And only when the ... *need* arises do I ... take to bathing." But, right she was, indeed, as Pilfree's head jerked back, like the recoil of a rifle, the shock of his long-denied odor smacking him in the nostrils. "Yes, well ... so, riddle me this. You have two U.S. coins totaling thirty-five cents. One of the coins, however, is not, I repeat, *not*, a quarter. What two U.S. coins do you have?"

Pilfree bent and plucked a blade of rye grass, confident of the stump factor his riddle presented. He inserted the blade between his lips, and, in a skillful dismissal of his hygienic shortcomings, he leaned against a nearby dogwood, arms folded against his chest, a slanted smirk of arrogance across his face.

"Two coins totaling thirty-five ... one's not a quarter ... what two ..." Taylor muttered, repeating the riddle's parts.

"Pilfree, you're such a *doofus!*" Bobbie Leigh said, shaking her head and turning her attention back to the document. "C'mon, Taylor, the *game*, remember?"

"I remember. Let me focus on this riddle for a minute. It's not like we're up against a *clock*, Bobbie Leigh. It just might help me with solving some of BJW's challenges."

"How are Pilfree's riddles going to help with *that?* Who can focus on *anything* wearing an orange-and-green plaid shirt, a pair of black-and-red striped overalls, and two blue-and-white-checkered tennis shoes staring *back* at you! Not to mention square-rimmed glasses big enough to frame pictures! And another thing ... what, wait ..." Bobbie Leigh leaned in close to Pilfree's face, her eyes squinted. She sighed. "Pilfree, there are no *lenses* in those frames."

"And your point is? Now, *hush up*, Bobbie Leigh Harwell! Let her focus."

Taylor snickered and turned from the distracting sight that was Pilfree Romulus Bojo and pondered the immediate challenge of his riddle.

"Give up, Taylor Smart?" Pilfree asked, nudging a poptart from its wrapper.

"Not *yet!*"

"Give *up* already, Taylor!" Bobbie Leigh urged. "The *game*."

"Okay, *okay*, I give. What two U.S. coins do I have?"

"A di-i-i-me ..." Pilfree said, extending the answer, giving Taylor a bit more time.

"Yes?"

"An-n-n-d–"

"–a *quarter!*" Taylor finished. "Ha!"

"But you said–" Bobbie Leigh started.

"What I said was that *one* of the coins was not a quarter. That coin would be–"

"The dime," Taylor said, smiling. "I get it, Pilfree. Good one."

"The ... the *dime?* But you said ... oh, yeah-h-h," Bobbie Leigh realized, her eyes brightening with the light only an epiphany could shine. "*Good* one, indeed, Pilfree. But make no mistake, my friend. You're still a doofus."

"Says *you!*" Pilfree replied. "And what do *you* know anyway, Bobbie Leigh?"

"Want to help us with a little game we're playing, Pilfree?" Taylor asked. "We just might be able to use you're insightful, riddle-busting, Rubikic abilities."

"Rubikic?" said Bobbie Leigh.

"A game?"

"Good idea, Muley! Yes, Pilfree, a game. A game of *challenges*. We have the first challenge right here; that is, if you think you're up to it."

"I don't know." Pilfree picked a fresh blade of rye grass, tucking it between his lips. He scratched his head. "Does this game involve a ball? You know, running or catching, *that* sort of game? 'Cause if it *does*, well–"

"What's that under your arm?" Bobbie Leigh asked, pointing her finger as if revealing a suspect.

"This? Box of poptarts, of course. Apple cinnamon. Want one, Bobbie Leigh Harwell? Two pastries give me one complete daily fruit serving. This box represents my version of an apple-a-day, times five!"

"Yuck! After where they've *been?* I don't think so!"

"No ball and no running, Pilfree," Taylor said.

"I don't know ..." Pilfree bit a corner off his poptart.

"C'mon, Pilfree. Three heads are better than two, even if one of 'em's the head of an unwashed *doofus*."

"Bobbie Leigh!" Taylor said.

"I'm just *kidding* him! Right, Pilfree?"

"If you say so, Bobbie Leigh Harwell," Pilfree replied, crumbs falling from his mouth.

"I say so, Pilfree. It'll be fun. C'mon!"

"Well ... okay. Why not? What do I have to do?"

"Not sure yet," Taylor replied. "Let's read the first challenge."

"What is this anyway?" Pilfree asked, pointing to the document. "I mean, it looks like vellum, but what's it say? And where'd you get it? And ... why are you here at Crepe Myrtle Hill, next to the grave of old man WonVillingham?"

Taylor and Bobbie Leigh shared the BJW letter with Pilfree, bringing him up to speed, and how it was discovered inside Taylor's antique radio.

"WonVillingham's dead, you know," Pilfree said.

"How do you know such as that?" Bobbie Leigh asked.

"Well, for one, here's his headstone."

"And for two?"

"I happen to know he went and died the Good Death." Pilfree's rye blade fell mangled to the ground.

"The ... what did you call it ... the *Good* Death?" Taylor asked.

"That's what I called it."

"What in the world is a *good* death?" asked Bobbie Leigh, "and since when's a death *ever* good, anyhow?"

"Not the death *itself*," Pilfree answered, "but the *way* in which one dies, surrounded by family and such. Least, that's what I heard."

"Since when do you hear *anything*, Pilfree Bojo! You probably made that up in one of your classroom daydreams!"

"Did *not!* WonVillingham's dead, all right!"

"Okay, so when did he die, and how was his death ... good," Taylor probed.

"Good for *me*, Taylor!" Bobbie Leigh answered. "If he's dead, then I'm *glad* for it!"

"Not that kind of good, Bobbie Leigh Harwell," Pilfree said.

"Then *what?*"

"As I heard it, folks in the nineteenth century—"

"In case you weren't aware, Pilfree," Bobbie Leigh interrupted, "we're living in the *twenty-first* century."

"Quiet, Bobby Leigh! Let me answer the question. Now, as I heard it, folks in the nineteenth century, particularly in the decades up to and including the War Between the States, *expected* a Good Death and planned to *die* a Good Death, as they called it. The 'good' part meant that the person dying would be surrounded by family so the act of dying wouldn't be as scary as it might otherwise be, and to provide a proper send-off."

"Send-off?"

"Bobbie Leigh, don't you ever read *anything?*"

"Not if I can help it."

"The dying would make his or her peace with his or her maker, and in the witness of familiar folks—family—and thus would have died ... a good death.

"Of course," Pilfree continued, "that sort of end-of-life tradition—a routine, if you will—was greatly disrupted during the War Between the States—"

"I always thought it was the *Civil War*," Bobbie Leigh interrupted again.

"Either term'll do," Taylor said. "Both sides called it by different names–"

"*Hush up! Both* of you! If you're wanting to *hear* about this, then let me *tell* it."

"Sorry!" both girls answered.

"What with soldiers getting shot on battlefields hundreds of miles from home, and then either dying on those fields or in some hospital surrounded by other soldiers dying ... well, these men just couldn't die the Good Death. Indeed, their deaths were scary at best."

"Interesting piece of history, Pilfree, but what's all this got to do with Blythington Jehosiphats WonVillingham?" Bobbie Leigh asked, frustration rising.

"WonVillingham died the Good Death, like I said."

"But how do you *know* he died, Pilfree?" Taylor asked. "Were *you* there when he died? Did *you* attend his funeral?"

"Well ... not exactly."

"Then, how do you know this?" Bobbie Leigh echoed. "And please realize, Pilfree, that so far you have succeeded only in frustrating us."

Pilfree thought for a moment, head rested in his palm. "Reckon I don't know; not for sure, anyhow. But I was *told* such!"

"By whom, Pilfree" Taylor asked.

"If somebody told you the earth would be hit by an asteroid tomorrow, you'd lay awake all night believing it was true!" Bobbie Leigh said.

"The Unique Antiques owner told me," Pilfree answered. "What's his name? Tried to sell my Daddy the same radio your Mama bought, Taylor."

"When was that?"

"A month ago, maybe six weeks. Wanted too much for it."

"And you believed him," asked Bobbie Leigh.

"What's not to believe? Here's his headstone. Why would anyone *not dead* put up a headstone?"

"People put up their headstones all the time, in preparation," Bobbie Leigh observed.

"Maybe so, but–"

"Pilfree Bojo, open your eyes!" Bobbie Leigh said. "It ain't got the date of death carved in it. How you came to be the master of the Rubik's Cube, *I'll* never know."

"Would take someone other than WonVillingham to carve the date," Pilfree speculated, "being dead, you know. Maybe that person never got around to taking care of that little detail."

Pilfree took a closer look, head still in hand and eyes squinted. He opened his left arm, the box of apple cinnamon poptarts falling into his right hand. Taking another out, he began to eat.

"So," Pilfree mumbled, crumbs flying from his lips like toasted confetti, "what's the first challenge?"

"Let's read it," Taylor said.

"Read it *aloud*, Taylor," Bobbie Leigh urged. "Makes it sound more ... you know, more *serious*."

"You're goofy, Bobbie Leigh Harwell." Pilfree said, returning an insult.

"Says the *master*," Bobbie Leigh replied. "And don't you *know* it's impolite to eat with your mouth full? Especially in a *cemetery!*"

"You mean, it's impolite to *talk* with your mouth full, don't you?"

"In your case, *both!*"

"Stop it, you two. I'll read it aloud." Taylor cleared her throat, but before reading, she paused. "So, Pilfree, are you in this game with us, or what? Can't say for sure, but I suspect you're still in the clear, commitment-wise, that is. So you still have a choice."

"I don't know, Taylor," Bobbie Leigh said. "He knows too much to *really* be in the clear, which is something I thought I'd *never* say about one Pilfree Romulus Bojo, knowing too much, that is."

"I don't think so, BL. He sort of walked up on this, not *knowing* he had a choice, not like we did."

"Well, he read the document. He knows *now*."

"If it's all the same to you girls," Pilfree said, pondering the ramifications of joining the game and looking off in the distance, "my ... stomach's telling me a snack awaits. Good luck with BJW, be he alive or dead, and with his game!"

"I thought you just *ate* your snack!" Bobbie Leigh said.

"That's ... that's just ... just *half* of it," Pilfree replied as he started his retreat down the hillside, hurdling headstones and throwing out an occasional chuckle. "Need milk to wash it down, you know."

"There goes the last word in fashion statements!" Bobbie Leigh shouted, fingers locked on top of her head, mocking Pilfree's choice of clothing and colors. "Okay, Tay, I'm ready. Got nothing else to do on a Saturday, so let's do *this!*"

Taylor smiled and knelt, securing the document's corners with pebbles, and read.

"'You have successfully managed the *first* challenge, which was accepting the Game and its rules, its risks and its rewards. Let's move on to challenge number–'"

"Look at that Pilfree," Bobbie Leigh interrupted, pointing toward a towering, but very dead, oak tree near the cemetery's entrance. "What's he doing climbing that old rot, anyhow?"

"Climbing?" Taylor said, looking.

"Hey, Pilfree!" Bobbie Leigh shouted. "Don't you know a lightning-killed tree when you see one? Don't be trying to climb that thing! You'll snap off a branch, an' *then* where will you be? On the ground, sprawled deader'n Georgia roadkill, *that's* where!"

"You're not the boss of me, Bobbie Leigh Harwell!"

"Why are you climbing that tree, Pilfree?" Taylor asked, hands cupped around her mouth. "Doesn't look like much of a climbin' tree to me."

"Looks a whole lot like a *rotten* tree!" Bobbie Leigh said.

"Just me bein' me, I reckon," came Pilfree's reply as he shimmied the slanted trunk to the lowest limb.

"Just you be careful!"

"Don't you worry about me, Taylor Smart."

"We *won't!*" Bobbie Leigh shouted.

She and Taylor resumed reading the second challenge.

"Plummeting plumage!" Pilfree shouted.

C-R-R-R-A-A-A-S-S-S-H-H!

The girls looked up. A hundred feet or so downhill, their line of sight–the same line of sight along which Pilfree had trotted–filled with the horizontal sprawl of an ancient oak tree. Huge limbs lay scattered like spikes of spilled toothpicks. Headstones and monuments rested crumbled and crushed like castles of sand.

"Pilfree!" the girls shouted. They eyed the document and each other. A gasp of horror rushed from their mouths as they made the connection.

Taylor and Bobbie Leigh ran down the slope, stumbling over the debris and searching frantically for Pilfree within the darkened reaches of crispy branches. Like spears, shreds of thick limbs punctured the ground.

"Pilfree!" Bobbie Leigh shouted. "*Pilfree!* Are you okay? Talk to us!"

Several anxious minutes passed, not a human sound heard.

Then, a shrilly voice shot from amid the jumble of wood as a figure emerged through the shuffle of leaves and limbs.

"Anybody want a pop tart?" Pilfree asked, brushing his overalls free of debris. "What's *left* of 'em, anyway."

"Pilfree!" Taylor shouted, following his voice. "Pilfree, where *are* you?"

"Here ... I think."

Pilfree emerged from a tangle of broken branches, his red curls intertwined with dead leaves, rotted wood, pieces of bark and twigs, but otherwise unscathed.

"I think all my pop tarts are busted," Pilfree observed turning the bent box upside down and watching chunks of the pastries tumble to the ground. "I also think I *will* play this game of yours after all. Looks as if I *am* committed, like it or not, and I'd rather *live* a while longer," he said, adjusting his square-rimmed, lens-less glasses, "you know, wait for one of those ... *good* deaths."

Taylor and Bobbie Leigh stared at each other, and then at Pilfree, all three turning their gazes slowly in the direction of the document, one corner flapping to a gentle breeze against the headstone of Blythington Jehosiphats WonVillingham.

7

Challenge of the Unknown

"What's it *say*, Taylor," Bobbie Leigh asked as she maneuvered for position looking over Taylor's shoulder. "What's the next challenge?"

Pilfree munched on broken apple cinnamon pop tart parts and flicked twigs off his shoulders, leaves off his overalls.

"It says ...," Taylor said as she lifted the folds of the vellum. "Says ... 'Welcome to challenge number two. You and your ... *two* friends–now, how did he know *that?*–are indeed capable, but each of you has strengths the others wish they had. Likewise, each of you has weaknesses the others are glad they do not possess. An underlying challenge woven into all the challenges is the necessity to recognize and to utilize your personal strengths in order to offset and put asunder the weaknesses of your colleagues, weaknesses that if unrecognized–and thus unremedied–will doom the success of your game.'"

"*What?*" Bobbie Leigh asked, looking at Pilfree. "You mean not only do I gotta watch out for me, but I gotta watch out for *you*, too? Sounds *too* much like *homework*!"

"Worse, Bobbie Leigh," said Taylor. "More like a final exam."

"And I *can't* cheat?"

"Play along, Bobbie Leigh," Taylor replied. "Now let me finish."

"I'm playin', I'm *playin'*."

Bobbie Leigh sat and sighed, her back against the headstone. She cleared her throat.

"*Quiet*, Pilfree," she said.

"But, I didn't–"

"So, to continue," Taylor said, "'Challenge number two is as follows: 'You must locate a stone of an unknown. Take its form or facsimile to Unique Antiques, place it against the storefront, and make a photograph. But, no digital photos.

Return the form or facsimile, along with the photo, to its location of origin.'"

"The stone of the unknown?" Pilfree asked, cupping his chin between his index finger and thumb.

"Not quite, Pilfree," Taylor corrected. "I know you listened, but there was an easy-to-miss detail."

"Of course I listened ... hey ... wait a minute ... you're *right*, Taylor!"

"Right about what?" Bobbie Leigh begged. "Guys! Right about *what!*"

"Calm down, Bobbie Leigh," Pilfree said. "Not *the* stone of *the* unknown."

"That's what *I* heard," Bobbie Leigh said.

"A stone of *an* unknown, Bobbie Leigh," Pilfree said. "Or a *facsimile*. Big difference."

"A stone of an unknown *what*? If it ain't known, how will we ever determine what he's referring to?" Bobbie Leigh asked, her frustration mounting. "Could be *any* stone, anywhere, that one there in the rock wall, for instance."

"Not likely."

"A *headstone*, then," Bobbie Leigh said.

"Seriously?"

"I'm beginning to see one of *your* weaknesses, Bobbie Leigh," Pilfree said as he inserted a poptart chunk into his mouth.

"Says *you*, Pilfree Romulus Bojo. You're a walking weakness, head to toe."

"Oh, yeah? Who won the district math bee last year, hmmm?"

"I don't think WonVillingham's referring to some unknown *thing*," Taylor asserted. "I think he *means* for us to quickly figure these clues out. Just gotta use our brains, is all." Taylor lifted her eyes in Bobbie Leigh's direction and continued, "If this were some unknown *object*, we could spend forever trying to find a needle in an endless haystack."

"What are you getting at, Taylor?" Bobbie Leigh asked.

"She's getting at saying that the *stone* is the object, but the unknown is something more like a ... a ..."

"Hush up, Pilfree!"

"No, Bobbie Leigh, Pilfree's on the right track."

Pilfree issued a smirk at Bobbie Leigh.

"The 'unknown' part is more of a label, a name, a *noun*. Not an adjective," Taylor observed.

"Like the Tomb of the *Unknowns*!" Pilfree said.

"Exactly," Taylor agreed.

"But, we have no such Tomb of the Unknowns here in Raventon," Bobbie Leigh said. "Reckon BJW wants us to fly to D.C.?"

"No, we don't, and I doubt he expects us to do *that*," said Taylor, folding the vellum paper and ribbon, "but we *do* have the answer to this clue." She smiled and looked at Pilfree, who returned the smile.

"*What!*" Bobbie Leigh shouted.

"Frustration," Pilfree said, patting Bobbie Leigh on her shoulder.

"*Frustration* is the answer?"

"Your *weakness*, Bobbie Leigh."

"The *answer*, Bobbie Leigh, is in the cemetery," Taylor said, "the *Confederate* cemetery. All those headstones that have the word 'Unknown' carved into them. All we gotta do is dig one up."

"So, I was *right*. It *is* a headstone."

"Well, yes ... I suppose you were right, after all, Bobbie Leigh," Pilfree admitted. "Always a first time for everything."

"And just how do you propose we do *that?*" Bobbie Leigh asked, "Dig up a Confederate headstone, I mean. Wallowing amongst a cave full of skulls and bones is one thing, but taking a headstone from a grave is quite another."

"I know," Taylor said, placing her hand on Pilfree's shoulder. "It *is.* But I'm sure the *strength* of our good poptart-fortified friend will handle that problem well enough."

Pilfree lifted a broken poptart to his lips. Eyes wide, he stood frozen by Taylor's words, the pastry slipping from his fingers and falling to the ground.

Bobbie Leigh huffed. "Don't count on it," she whispered.

"Let's meet back here tonight, say nine o'clock," Taylor instructed. "I'll bring the shovel. Pilfree, you bring an old sheet. Bobbie Leigh, you bring the camera. Make sure it's a *film* camera, no digitals. Think your dad might have one somewhere?"

"He's pure digital. I do have one of those *Polaroid* cameras," Bobbie Leigh said, "the kind that spits out the pictures, develops it while you wait."

"We *know* the kind, Bobbie Leigh."

"Hush up, you ... you *Pilfree!*"

"Any film left in it?" Taylor asked.

"I'm not sure. I remember taking pictures with it once upon a time, but it probably has a couple inches of dust on it by now."

"Bring it. All we need is one picture."

"One more problem," Pilfree added.

"Do tell," Bobbie Leigh said.

"Headstones are big. And headstones are *heavy*."

"And *that* is why *you* are such an *important* part of this team, Pilfree!" Taylor said with a smile.

Pilfree clipped his thumbs to his suspenders and puffed out his chest, chin pointed high, a grin of agreement from ear to ear. Then, his chest sunk.

"*Now* what, doofus!"

"You ... you want me to bring a *sheet*? To a *cemetery*? Isn't that sort of like bringing a zombie to a family reunion?

"Sheets aren't ghosts, doofus," Bobbie Leigh said.

"To wrap the headstone in, Pilfree," Taylor said.

"Of course," he acknowledged. "What other reason would one need for bringing a sheet into the welcoming arms of a cemetery? I knew that."

8

The Headstone

"Where *is* he," Taylor asked, buttoning her sweater to turn away the chill.

"Probably scanning the skies for some undiscovered star," Bobbie Leigh replied with a sigh.

"Here I am," Pilfree said, his moving silhouette bobbing like the undead amid the tilted obelisks. "Had to shimmy that iron fence, the one with the equally iron points on top. Almost impaled myself."

"Gate's not locked, Pilfree," Taylor said.

"It isn't? I thought they locked–"

"Well, they didn't this time," Bobbie Leigh blurted.

"There's that frustration again," Pilfree observed.

"*You're* my frustration."

"Did you bring the sheet?" Taylor asked.

"Got it right here, in my handy-dandy backpack. Got my *muscles* on, too."

Bobbie Leigh rolled her eyes. "*That'll* be the day. I do wish you'd put on a different pair of pants. And *sneakers*. Those have *got* to be—"

"Let's get moving," Taylor interrupted, ever vigilant to keep the team focused. "Over here."

The headstone selected rested at a roughly thirty-degree tilt in the ground at the end of a silent row of dozens of similar slabs of stones. Taylor shone her flashlight on the granite slab. Arced across its gray-white weathered face was carved the word 'UNKNOWN'. Nothing more. The three stood in silent respect, staring at the word.

"Definitely *not* a Good Death," Pilfree mumbled.

"Wonder who it was," Bobbie Leigh said.

"Not how I want to be remembered," Taylor added.

H-H-Hooo-Hooo-Hoo.

"What was—"

"Just an owl, Pilfree."

"That's a *real* owl?" Pilfree asked. "I thought they only put owls in *movie* cemeteries."

"Smile for the camera, Pilfree," Bobbie Leigh teased, pointing her Polaroid at Pilfree.

"Bobbie Leigh, keep your eyes on that gate for anybody coming," Taylor said. "Pilfree, you jiggle the headstone back and forth while I dig around the base."

"Yeah, Pilfree, pretend it's one of your oversized teeth."

"Ain't this against the law, what we're doing?" Pilfree asked.

"Of *course* not," Taylor said. "Well, *sort* of. Okay, *yes*, it is. Except we'll be bringing this stone back, just as soon as we deliver it to Unique Antiques and photograph it."

"That might take all night, Taylor," Bobbie Leigh said. "How heavy you reckon that thing is?"

"Too heavy for one, but just right for three," Taylor answered, pushing the shovel blade into the soil. "Jiggle it."

"Won't jiggle. Dig some more," Pilfree said. "Need us a jackhammer and a wheelbarrow."

"This thing must go deeper than I thought," Taylor said. She stepped on the shovel's blade, pushing it a few inches into the moistened soil. "*Now* jiggle it."

"Nothing, Taylor," Pilfree said. "Here, give me that shovel."

Pilfree plunged the blade into the cut already made by Taylor.

"Wait a minute!" Taylor said as she unfolded the vellum. "Stop digging, Pilfree."

"Stop dig–?"

"Listen up. Says here, blah, blah, blah ... right here ... 'Take its *form* or *facsimile* to Unique Antiques, place it against the storefront, and make a photograph. No digital photos. Return *the form* or *facsimile* to its location of origin.'"

"So?" Bobbie Leigh asked, watching for intruders.

"Its *form*, Bobbie Leigh."

"O-o-o ... kay. It's a form all right. A heavy form at that, if y'all ever get it dug up."

"*Think*, Bobbie Leigh."

"Don't ask the impossible, Taylor," Pilfree said, chuckling.

"Taylor, the instructions told us that we have to follow the *letter* of the challenges, no exceptions," Bobbie Leigh said as she gave Pilfree the evil eye.

"To the letter, yes, but it *also* said we could use the tools of our *imagination*, that there were *multiple* paths to the correct solutions."

"What other solution could there be, other than what we're doing now?" Pilfree asked. "We have to take the stone—"

"Give me your camera, Bobbie Leigh," Taylor instructed.

"My camera? But it's only got a couple a shots left. What are you going to do, Taylor?"

"This," Taylor said, lifting the camera to her eye and pushing the button. A pop of light illuminated the cemetery. Taylor grabbed the photograph as it slid out the slot.

"Great. Now we have only *one* shot left," Bobbie Leigh said.

"Think you can carry *this?*" Taylor tossed the picture to Pilfree.

"I *get* it," Pilfree said, the epiphany rising. "By George, you are *brilliant*, Taylor Smart! This is a *form* of the stone, a *photo facsimile* of the stone! WonVillingham never intended for us to actually *remove* a headstone. You've spared me from having to show off my extraordinary muscular prowess, and I thank you."

Bobbie Leigh smiled. "Gotta hand it to you, Muley. You *do* have a way with brilliance. And she spared you from the embarrassment of a hernia, Pil-boy."

"Let's take this photo to the shop, set it in front of the door, and photograph *it*," Taylor said.

"A photograph of a photograph," Bobbie Leigh whispered. "What'll she think of next!"

"Don't forget," Pilfree noted, "we'll need to bring *that* photo back here."

"Now *this* is what I call teamwork!" Bobbie Leigh said, hands on hips.

"Spoken like a true spectator," Pilfree teased.

"Don't forget, Your Pil-ness, 'twas *I* who first suggested the idea of a headstone."

"I'm sure you'll see to it neither of us *ever* forgets."

9

Not Even A Drop!

Back in the cemetery, Taylor leaned the photograph of the photograph against the base of the headstone.

"Nice photo, Bobbie Leigh," Taylor remarked. You managed to get the shop's name in the picture, too. Proof positive."

"And only one chance to get it right."

"Okay, so what's the *next* challenge?" Pilfree asked, pinching his arms and neck. "I see we're all *still* alive."

"And you're *still* a doofus," Bobbie Leigh added.

Taylor pulled the vellum from her sweater pocket, unfolded it, and began reading challenge number three.

"Says here, 'Your third challenge is to retrieve your fourth challenge.' Okay. That sounds simple enough."

"*What?* What kind of challenge is *that?*" Bobbie Leigh asked, again her frustration showing through.

"Is there more, Taylor?" Pilfree asked.

"There's more. Says 'Proceed to Zebulon's Crossing. Cross the river without the use of any bridge, man-made or otherwise, or any manner of flotation device (including boats, rafts, tires, levitation).'"

"*No* levitation?" Pilfree said. "I was sort of *counting* on that. What about teleportation?"

"Let her read the challenge!"

Taylor took a breath and continued. "'Most importantly, you must cross the river without getting a single drop of water on your person or clothing."

"How will *he* know whether or not we get a drop of water *on our person or clothing*? He's *dead*, for Pete's sake." Bobbie Leigh asked, rolling her eyes.

"The spirit and eyes of Blythington Jehosiphats WonVillingham are *everywhere*," Pilfree said in his best Bela Lugosi.

"As is your doofusness," Bobbie Leigh replied.

"Let me *finish*, guys!" Taylor begged. "'There is an oak tree on the other side of the river. You will know this tree by a large, irregular tumor of wood around its trunk, on which you will find a knothole.'"

"Found me a knothole right here," Bobbie Leigh said, pointing, "right here in Pilfree's knot*head*."

Taylor sighed and continued reading. "Inside the knothole will be Challenge number four. And you thought Challenge number three was easy."

"*Easy?* Crossing the river without a bridge or boat, without any water touching our person or clothing? That's *easy?*" Pilfree said.

"Without a *drop* of water touching *our person or clothing,*" Bobbie Leigh added.

"I just *said* that."

"You left out the word 'drop'. Besides, who listens to *you!*"

Pilfree had never crossed so much as a narrow creek, unless by bridge, any of which, by the way, he was most afraid. The entirety of his childhood had been spent void of the carefree splashings in rain puddles, even the pleasure of cooling dips in swimming pools. Crossing rivers without the aid of a sturdy steel-and-concrete bridge, in the darkness of night, no less, seemed to him beyond the possible and sent his mind reeling.

"Does sound pretty difficult, Taylor," Bobbie Leigh observed. "Even for you."

"We have to work *together*, guys," Taylor reminded them. "That's the whole point. These challenges are designed to make us *think*. But like the headstone challenge, the solution is probably right in front of our noses."

"All I see in front of *my* nose is darkness," Bobbie Leigh said. "Maybe we should wait until morning, until we have some *real* light."

"That'll attract too much attention," Taylor said. "Folks'll get in our way, ask too many questions, take away our focus. Get us wet. We can't afford distractions or mistakes."

"Or *what?* We'll all *die?*" Bobbie Leigh asked, feigning concern, hands clasped together at her face.

"She's right," Pilfree agreed. "Can't afford distractions. We'd better get on to Zebulon's Crossing. But remember, we can *not* take the bridge across."

"It's shallow enough there to *walk* across," Bobbie Leigh said.

"Can't get wet, remember?" Taylor reminded Bobbie Leigh. "Not even a little."

"Who's the doofus *now?*" Pilfree asked.

"Not even a *drop*," Taylor said.

"So, we're leaving the photo of a photo here, against this Confederate headstone?" Bobbie Leigh asked.

"Suppose so," Taylor replied.

"What if I stay behind and watch to see who retrieves the photo," Pilfree suggested.

"That'll be like watching a glacier melt," Bobbie Leigh answered. "He won't show up."

"I guess you're right. But don't make it a habit, being right, that is. I like you the way you are," Pilfree said with a mischievous wink. Bobbie Leigh ignored the remark.

"How do you think we'll be able to pull this off, Muley?" Bobbie Leigh asked.

Taylor reached inside her backpack. "With this .... BL."

"A *rope?*" Bobbie Leigh asked. "Who *are* you, anyway? *Dora the Explorer?* You brought a *rope?*"

"Looks that way, Bobbie Leigh," Pilfree said. "Even *I* can tell it's a rope."

"Hush up! I *know* it's a rope, but how'd you think to *bring* it?"

"Actually, I must confess I didn't think to bring it. I just ... always keep a rope in my backpack."

"Since the cave thing, I'm guessing?" Bobbie Leigh said.

"I dunno; yeah, I suppose. I just sort of figured it would come in handy some day, *especially* since our adventures in the chamber of skulls."

"A bit skinny, this rope," Pilfree observed, running his fingers along its length. "And light."

"But strong, too," Taylor said. "Just hope it's *long* enough."

"How long *is* it?"

"Fifteen, twenty feet, give or take. River looks to be only about twenty feet wide at Zeb's. More a creek than a river. This is where your math-mind will come in handy, Pilfree."

"We're *doomed*," Bobbie Leigh said.

"We're *not* doomed, Bobbie Leigh!" Pilfree said. "I won the math bee, don't you know."

"How could we forget?"

"I reckon you got a *Swiss Army knife,* too, in that backpack of yours?" Pilfree asked.

Taylor reached inside, pulling out a Swiss Army knife.

"Wow," Bobbie Leigh said, "if you're ever on Let's Make A Deal–!"

"Okay," Pilfree said, scratching his head. "So, how do you propose we *use* this rope?"

"Well," Taylor answered, hesitancy on her lips, "I've been to Zebulon's Crossing a time or two, family picnics and hiking. River's not only *shallow* there, it also narrows enough for one to ... well ... *swing* across."

"*Swing* across?" Pilfree said, releasing his grip on his poptart box, the contents scattering.

"I think that's probably the only way we can keep from getting wet," Taylor replied. "I'll entertain other ideas, but we aren't allowed to float across or use bridges. Or teleportation devices. Wouldn't be much of a challenge if we *could*, you know. Besides, rules of the game."

"Assuming we can hold our grip," Pilfree said. "Assuming the rope doesn't break; assuming whatever we tie the rope *to* doesn't break; assuming the rope's long enough; assuming one of you can tie a decent knot with this thing; assuming–"

"Life is full of assumptions, Pilfree. Just gotta make sure that we find a tree *tall* enough," Taylor said as she looked for comparable examples with the trees surrounding them, "and close enough to the bank's edge, one with a limb sturdy enough to hold this rope *and* our body weights.

"Limb's gotta hang out over the river, the sturdy part at least midway across," Taylor continued. "I picture it—the point where we tie the rope around the tree limb and the two points of the opposite banks—as forming an equilateral triangle, more or less, giving us the ability to swing across without getting wet."

"Who needs Pilfree," Bobbie Leigh said, laughing, "when Taylor's already figured this out.

"Not sure I have it *all* figured out, Bobbie Leigh," Taylor answered. "Mine is more of an abstract perception of what's needed. Pilfree will have to determine how much rope is used in tying the knot, which has to be based on his estimate of the *width* of the river and *height* of the limb. The limb's strength has to extend out to at least half the river's width. Height of the limb from the river's surface has got to be very close to equaling the width of the river. When we swing across, the rope cannot touch the water, and it has to carry us all the way to the other side, on our *first* attempts. This challenge has *very little* room for error."

"Sounds complicated. Aren't there boulders in the river at Zebulon's Crossing, shoals and stuff?" Bobbie Leigh asked. "Why not just *walk* across?"

"We could try that, I guess," Taylor replied. "Comes down to which grip you think you're more apt to lose, your hands or your feet. Besides, if they've opened the dam upstream, water could be splashing over those rocks."

Bobbie Leigh and Pilfree looked at each other. They looked at each other's shoes.

"Taylor, do you really believe our *lives* are in danger if we fail to follow the rules of a challenge?" Bobbie Leigh asked. "I mean, what can *possibly* happen to us?"

"Can't know for sure, Bobbie Leigh," Taylor answered. "It's the domain of possibilities that scares me, though. You saw what happened to Pilfree and that tree back at the cemetery. Coincidence? Maybe, probably. But I'm not much of a believer in coincidence. And I don't think I'm quite ready to put Mr. WonVillingham, dead or alive, to the test."

"Pilfree, those checkered monstrosities covering your feet can hardly grip the *ground*," Bobbie Leigh said, pointing to his sneakers. "I wouldn't trust 'em on water-slicked rocks if I were you. Me, I'm going with the rope, and I suggest you do the same."

Pilfree lifted his feet and stared at the soles of his blue-and-white checkered sneakers. Brushing away blades of wet grass, he issued a sigh. "Looks like we have a river to swing."

10

Zebulon's Crossing

"How'd it get it's name," Pilfree asked.

"How'd who get *what's* name?" Bobbie Leigh replied.

"More like how'd *what* get *whose* name," Pilfree replied. "This crossing of Zebulon's, *that's* what?"

"Look for a tree, y'all," Taylor urged, moving the beam of her flashlight over the terrain along the river bank. "And watch for snakes."

"*Snakes?*" Bobbie Leigh said, eyes trained upon the ground.

"That time of year," Taylor replied.

"Probably one of Raventon's founder's?" Pilfree suggested, looking at trees.

"Indeed, it was," Taylor replied. "In 1803, Zebulon Franklin selected this site for a ferry and trading post."

"How do you know all this stuff, Taylor?" Bobbie Leigh asked.

"Any relation to Benjamin?" Pilfree asked.

"Library," Taylor answered. "They have books there, remember?"

"Nobody uses the *library* anymore," Pilfree said. "Google, Kindle, and a comfy couch."

"I still use libraries, Pilfree," Taylor said. "I like the feel of a solid book in the palms of my hands. I like the sound of real pages turning. And I *don't* like shortcuts."

"Computers aren't shortcuts–"

"*There,* Pilfree!" said Taylor in a whispered shout. "Our tree?"

Maybe fifty feet downstream from the bridge at Zebulon's Crossing, an oak tree tilted toward the river, its venerable branches twisting and angling like skeletal fingers over the water.

"Looks to be a twenty-degree slant, I'd say," Pilfree said. "Shine the light on the branches, Taylor. Let's see what we have to work with."

"Can you shimmy that thing, Pilfree?" Taylor asked.

"Keep my poptarts dry and I'll shimmy *anything.*"

"Will you *lose* those blasted poptarts, already!" Bobbie Leigh said. "And how is it you *never* seem to run out of 'em?"

"Me being me."

"That limb there looks pretty sturdy," Taylor said, pointing. "We'll give you a boost, Pilfree."

Taylor and Bobbie Leigh cupped their hands, their fingers interlocked. Pilfree placed one foot into the hold. On a count of three, the girls lifted Pilfree within reach of a limb low enough to firmly grasp. Pilfree pulled himself up, pressing the trunk with his feet for leverage. He made his way to the branch that would serve as the base for the rope.

"How's it feel, Pilfree?" Taylor asked.

"Strong," he replied, as he held tightly to a higher branch and slide-stepped his way forward on the limb, "but it *thins* ahead considerably—"

C-R-R-R-A-A-A-C-C-K-K-K

"Not a good sound, Pilfree!" Bobbie Leigh said.

"Sounds like you've already reached thin," Taylor said. "Back away!"

"Agreed!" Pilfree replied, shuffling backwards a couple of feet. "Is this far enough out over the water, Taylor? To hang the rope?"

"Looks to be," Taylor replied, shining the flashlight on the point of the limb and from bank to bank. "I'll toss the rope over the branch. You stay put."

Taylor tossed, and the rope fell across the branch. Pilfree double-looped one end around the branch and knotted it firmly, testing it with three quick pulls.

"Grab the rope, Taylor, both hands," Pilfree instructed. "Lift your feet off the ground and hang a minute to see if the knot is secure," Pilfree said.

"And to see if the branch'll hold," Taylor replied, lifting her feet, wrapping her legs around the rope, and pulling herself up a few feet. "Feels ... tight, and there's enough on this end to ... tie around our waists, in case our hands slip. Gotta make sure our bottoms ... don't skim the water as we're swinging across."

"You okay, Taylor?" Pilfree asked, sensing distress in her voice.

"I think so," Taylor replied, struggling to get air. "A little tired, I guess. Not used to that sort of exertion, maybe."

"Wait a minute," Bobbie Leigh said. "Tie the rope around our *waists*? How am I gonna drop to the other side if the rope's tied to my waist?"

"I hate to admit it, Taylor," Pilfree said, "but she's got a point."

"Yep, and a good point at that," Taylor replied. "I'm thinking safety, but that would only make the possible impossible."

"And doom the game," Bobbie Leigh added.

"So, you gotta a tape measure in that backpack of yours, Taylor?" Pilfree asked.

"Think so," Taylor replied, rummaging her hand inside the pack. "Right here."

"Toss it to me."

"What if you lose your balance and plop right into that water, Pilfree?" shouted Bobbie Leigh.

"Always looking on the bright side, aren't you? What if I *do*, Bobbie Leigh? Best I can hope for is that my splash gets *you* wet, too."

"What're you going to do with the tape measure, Pilfree?" Taylor asked as she underhanded the device to Pilfree.

Pilfree took hold of the tape and pulled out several feet of its length.

"Catch this, Taylor," he said, tossing the container end of the tape measure toward her. "Now hold it against the end of the rope," Pilfree instructed. "Pull the rope tight. What's the rope's length?"

Taylor held the tape container end against the rope and shone her flashlight. "Twenty-one feet, three and a quarter inches," she replied.

Pilfree paused a minute or so, taking a penny from his pocket. "I'm guessing I'm fifteen or sixteen feet above the water." He dropped the penny. "Nope. seventeen feet. That leaves a bit more than four feet to make grips for our hands and feet. I suggest first tying a couple of knots about a yard apart, something to grab hold of with our hands and feet as we swing."

"Did you drop something into the water?" Bobbie Leigh asked.

"A penny, if you must know."

"Why'd you drop a penny? To confirm gravity?"

"I was sort of hoping you'd dive in after it. Actually, to estimate the distance, that's why."

Taylor worked the two knots, having learned the skills of knot-tying in Girl Scouts and from her dad.

"How does *that* help you tell the distance, Pilfree Romulus Bojo?" Bobbie Leigh persisted, nibbling on one of Pilfree's poptarts. "By the way, you might be a doofus, but you're pretty smart when it comes to poptart flavors."

"Experience, Bobbie Leigh. Experience." Pilfree slid down the slanted trunk to the ground. "And I did a quick mental calculation of distance based on the time it took the penny to hit the water, something you wouldn't understand. Hey, nice knotting, Taylor. Bank looks high enough there to get a running start."

"It better be," Taylor said, pulling the rope and examining all factors.

"Think we have enough rope to swing us far enough?" Bobbie Leigh asked.

"Only one way to find out," Taylor replied. "I'm relying on Pilfree's experience in distance-judging.

"And your skills with knot-tieing."

"So, who's first?" Taylor asked.

Bobbie Leigh and Pilfree cleared their throats and brushed nonexistent debris from their hair.

"Guess *I'm* first," Taylor answered herself. "I'll need a good push from one of you."

"*You* push, Pilfree," Bobbie Leigh said. "I'll pray.

Taylor pulled herself to grasp the highest rope knot, wrapping her feet around the low knot. She stood erect and sighed.

"Ready?" asked Pilfree.

"As I'll ever be."

"Question," Bobbie Leigh said. "How will you get the rope back to this side?"

Taylor stopped and thought. "Good question."

"And from Bobbie Leigh," Pilfree said. "She's two for two. Who'd-a thunk it?"

"I could sling it," Taylor replied after some thought, "but that might not be good enough. If you didn't catch it, it would just flop around until it settled hanging from the branch over the middle of the river."

"If it did, Taylor, I could climb the tree, scoot out on the limb and retrieve the rope," Pilfree said.

"But I'd have the flashlight, Pilfree, not you. I need the light to guide my landing. There's too much foliage to get enough light from across the river shining on you up on that limb. Besides, you might finish breaking the limb."

"So use the flashlight to get the rope back to this side," Pilfree suggested.

"How is *that* going to work?" Bobbie Leigh asked.

"Must we explain *everything* to you?"

"For one thing," Taylor said, "it'll give me something with some *weight*, to tie to the rope and swing back across to you guys. It'll help stabilize the direction and flight of the rope."

"You are so *brilliant*, Taylor!" Bobbie Leigh observed.

"Credit goes to Pilfree," Taylor said, stepping up the embankment's side pocked with erosion and taking a deep breath. "Okay. Let's do this. When I say 'go', Pilfree, you give me a booster shove as I run past you, hard as you can. On three."

Pilfree took his position. Bobbie Leigh closed her eyes, lips muttering in prayer. Taylor made ready.

"One!" she shouted, "Two ... *Three!*"

Taylor came charging forward, determination on her face, and as she passed, Pilfree lunged forward with outstretched hands, ready to add to her momentum. Instead, he shoved the empty air, missing her entirely. Taylor raised her legs, bent at the knees, and began her swing across the Sagitaw River. The branch quivered, showering leaves as it released decades of pent-up creaks. Bobbie Leigh and Pilfree watched, almost expecting the branch to snap.

The branch held.

The distance was just as Pilfree had measured it to be, with a couple of inches to spare. As the rope's swing took her over the river, Taylor instinctively gripped the knots tighter with her hands and feet. She kept the flashlight pressed between her hands and the rope, its beam brightening her approach. Sailing over the opposite bank, she loosened her firm grip at just the right second. Her palms slid down a couple feet of the rope, her shoes dragging the sandy soil. She felt the cutting burn of the rope between her thumbs and forefingers, but retained her grip while sticking the landing any gymnast might boast of.

"Am I alive?" she shouted. "Rope burn!"

"Very much so, Taylor," Pilfree answered. "Tie the flashlight to the rope and swing it back."

"Doing it," Taylor said, bending down. "Let me cool my hands off first."

"Taylor, *no!*" shouted Pilfree.

Taylor froze, inches away from the water's cooling touch.

"Oops," she said. "Thanks, Pilfree. Wasn't thinking."

"Probably wouldn't matter at this point, Taylor," Pilfree said. "You've satisfied the requirements stipulated in crossing the river. But best not to take uncertain risks."

"Throwing the rope back at you."

"Okay, so who's next?" Bobbie Leigh asked, looking at Pilfree as he caught the rope.

"Um, maybe you should go next, Bobbie Leigh," Pilfree said grabbing hold of the rope-tied flashlight.

"Why *me?*"

"Here's why: I'm heavier than you. If I go and the limb snaps, how will you get across?"

"Pilfree, if the limb snaps, you'll fall into the river."

Pilfree stared at Bobbie Leigh. "Yes, and your point is?"

"You realize you're just adding to your doofusness, don't you?" Bobbie Leigh said.

Pilfree continued the stare. "So I'll fall into the river. It's shallow enough to walk through, even if I do get completely–"

Bobbie Leigh tilted her head, arms folded.

"–wet. Oh yeah," he said. "Game over. For me."

"For you. For me. For Taylor."

"So, how're we gonna do this?"

"Flip a coin?"

"Heads," Pilfree said.

Bobbie Leigh pulled a dime from her pocket and flipped the coin into the air. Catching it, she turned it onto her forearm.

"Tails. See ya, doofus. And don't foul this up."

Pilfree looked at the rope in his hands. He yanked it a couple of times. The branch creaked in response to his pulls. A twig of leaves fell onto his head.

"Me and trees ... recent history's *not* so good," he said.

Pilfree turned to a series of exposed rocks, shoals that spanned the river's width. All the rocks appeared to have dry surfaces and with any luck–and a lot of care–could be stepped without touching the water. But, unlike the tread of Pilfree's sneakers, not all of the boulders were flat.

"You're not going to do what I think you're *about* to do," Bobbie Leigh said.

"Why not?"

"Pilfree, your sneakers are like greased hands. You won't make it over the first rock."

"I know these sneakers don't seem up to the task, Bobbie Leigh, but I believe that branch has only one good swing left in it."

"But, Pilfree ..."

"I'm too heavy." Pilfree handed Bobbie Leigh the rope and tapped the first boulder with his sneaker. "This is my best chance. The last good swing is yours."

"Y'all coming or not?" Taylor said. "I think I've found the knot-holed oak."

"Pilfree's gonna walk the rocks across!"

"Pilfree! Your *shoes!*"

"It'll be ... okay, Taylor" Pilfree replied. He placed his full weight on the first boulder. "Good and firm," he whispered. "Not so bad."

Each boulder rested more or less a foot apart, the surfaces perhaps three inches above the water's flow. Moss-like growth covered several of the boulders.

"Here, Pilfree. You'll need this," Bobbie Leigh said, extending her arm.

"The flashlight. Indeed," Pilfree said, taking it. "Remember to get a good running start with the rope."

Bobbie Leigh gazed at the rope and considered the rock option. "I appreciate your concern in giving me the last good swing of the rope, Pil-boy, but I'm right behind you," she said.

Pilfree steadied himself. Stepping forward, one shoe took a slight slide on the rock's slime cover, tipping his balance. The bottom of his left sneaker grazed the river's surface. "Not on my person," he said, retaining his balance as Bobbie Leigh winced. "Let me ... let me get a couple of rocks ahead of you. Then I'll shine the light toward the next rock ahead of *you*. Step to that rock, and then I'll step to the next rock ahead of me. Then I'll shine the light back–"

"I *get* it, Pilfree. Just *go!*"

"Y'all be careful," Taylor shouted. "I need that light to check out this knothole."

"Coming, Taylor," Pilfree replied.

"If not going," Bobbie Leigh added.

11

Hewlett-Packard of Its Day

Pilfree stepped ashore, proud of–if not surprised by–his evolving team skills; proud, too, of his ability to face his doubts; and proud of his shoes for holding up to the task, in spite of his clumsiness.

Bobbie Leigh followed, careful to avoid a misstep on the slick mud of the river bank's incline, the irony of such carelessness that would send her sliding into the water. She turned and gazed toward the other side, at the silent tree bearing the odd view of a dangling rope hanging above the river, like the debris of an Allied crossing. She stood, knees a bit wobbly from the muscle-tightening experience of walking mossy river rocks in the dark of night, glad still she'd not taken the rope. Challenges, choices, and teamwork. Blythington Jehosiphats WonVillingham's game was just warming up.

"That the tree?" Pilfree asked.

"Think so," Taylor replied, standing at the base of the barkless tree. "Looks deader'n night. Point the flashlight on that knothole, there."

Pilfree shone the light at the knothole. The wood inside the hole seemed alive with a quivering black mass of movement.

"And so, there it is," Taylor whispered, "as promised."

Challenge number four lay smack in the middle, protruding amid hundreds of parts that guided the quivering whole, now stirred by the intrusion of light, sound, and a probing stick.

"Yikes!" shouted Bobbie Leigh. "What in the name of Rasputin ..."

"Just carpenter ants," Taylor replied.

"*Ants?*" Pilfree asked.

"They won't hurt you, Pilfree," Taylor said. "Much, anyway. It's not like they're *fire* ants. Harmless as ... butterflies. Probably."

"I'm so reassured," Bobbie Leigh said.

"Butterflies with *stingers!*" Pilfree added.

"The only *harmless* ant," Bobbie Leigh said, "is a *dead* ant."

Taylor sighed. "Hold this," she said, handing the flashlight to Pilfree. She reached her hand into the middle of the black quiver and pulled out the rolled document. She shook free the ants. "See?" she said, flicking away one crawling up her forearm. "Harmless."

"Those things give me the *shudders*," Pilfree observed.

"*Daylight* gives *you* the shudders," Bobbie Leigh teased with a roll of her eyes.

"What's challenge number four, Taylor?" Pilfree asked, eluding Bobbie Leigh's lighthearted jab.

"It says, 'Identify this object and its usefulness.'" Taylor unfolded an attached piece of paper. "What the ...!"

"What is it, Taylor?" Pilfree asked. "Let's see!"

Pilfree took the paper. "Wow! Looks like a picture of the steering wheel on my dad's '67 Camaro. Only a *lot* rustier. And pukier green."

"*Pukier* green? Let me see that," Bobbie Leigh said, grabbing the paper from Pilfree's hand. "Light, please."

Taylor tilted the flashlight onto the photo.

"Ant!" Bobbie Leigh shouted.

Taylor flicked away the ant.

"Thanks. Looks like a steering wheel to me, too," she said, handing the document back to Taylor. "Now what?"

"This is no steering wheel," Taylor said, rotating and tilting the photo in multiple directions, trying to gain a bit of a three-dimensional perspective.

"Yeah?" asked Pilfree. "How can you tell? We've only got this picture, and it sure *looks* Camaro-ish to me."

"Because a '67 Camaro steering wheel has only *three* spokes, not four," Taylor answered. "Besides, this wheel seems too flat in relation to its spokes. And how do you explain those round objects *between* the spokes?"

"What makes you such an authority on Camaros?"

"'Cause my dad *owned* a '67, once upon a mid-life crisis. He'd let me ride in his lap, hold the wheel, and I'd pretend to steer."

"Sounds dangerous," Pilfree said.

"Not if it's driveway driving."

"So what *are* those other round objects between the spokes, Taylor?" Bobbie Leigh asked.

"They look something like circular saw disks, but *that* doesn't make sense," Taylor answered.

"*Nothing* about this game makes sense."

"Granted."

"So, remind me *why* we're playing this game," Bobbie Leigh said.

"Why not play?" Taylor answered. "Other kids go on vacations, to summer camps, cruises to exotic tropical locales. Who needs any of that when we can spend our summer playing games filled with life-or-death challenges. Life on the edge is why we play. The reward incentive ain't bad, either."

"Can't we just hike the Grand Canyon or the Appalachian Trail?"

"And do what countless others have already done?"

"Beats life-or-death. I'd rather not have to choose between the two. Besides, I'm having to retake algebra this summer. Isn't that death-defying enough?"

"Everything we do in this life is a choice between the two, Bobbie Leigh, when you strip away all the clutter. Even Grand Canyon hikes."

"Gears, maybe?" Pilfree offered, holding the picture between the girls' faces.

"*What*, Pilfree!" Bobbie Leigh said. "Can't you see we're having a conversation here!"

"Sorry," Pilfree replied. "But the game. And this object. Looks like a lot of teeth on gears?"

"Let's check out the clue, which, by the way," Taylor said, "reads more like a limerick or a riddle."

"Read it aloud."

"Like I would read it *silently*, Bobbie Leigh?"

Swishing away another black ant, Taylor read the battered paper:

"Once upon a watered wheel
long sleeping in the depths

no longer turned its teeth now still,
long hardened 'cross its breadth.

"What first was Greek, was put a-sail
from Greece to Syracuse;
technology as none had known
a thousand years they'd lose.

"When this device was in its prime
its center was the Earth;
eclipses of the sun and moon
its military worth.

"The Hewlett-Packard of its day,
precision in each turn;
first determine what this is,
for the sealed note you must earn."

Taylor sighed, staring at the challenge with the same stupefying confusion a pig might experience staring at a smart phone.

"That's *it?*" Bobbie Leigh said. "A stupid *poem?*"

"Seems that way, BL," Taylor replied.

"How're we supposed to figure out what it means?"

"What 'sealed note'?" Pilfree asked.

"I ... don't know," Taylor said, turning the photo 270 degrees. "Wait, here it is, in this envelope taped to the back of the challenge."

Taylor peeled off the tape. The envelope, its size about that of a 'Thank-You' card, was sealed in reddish-burgundy wax and imprinted with the initials BJW.

"Open it, Taylor!" Bobbie Leigh said.

"Don't think so, BL."

"Why not?"

"Says *not* to, right here," Taylor answered, pointing to the scribbling underneath the wax. "Says, 'This sealed note you must earn. Open only after you have solved the riddle of the poem. Herein is part B of Challenge 4.'"

"Part *B?* But, we–"

"For the sealed note you must earn," Pilfree said. "Remember the poem?"

"Earn? Earn *how?*"

"Well, Bobbie Leigh," Taylor replied, "first we have to figure out what the poem is talking about."

"You call *that* a poem?" Bobbie Leigh said. "More like gibberish, if you ask me."

"No one's asking you," Pilfree said.

"Lots of clues in that 'gibberish', BL," Taylor said. "It's up to us to decipher them, so we can move ahead to the message in the envelope."

"Let me see that poem, Taylor," Pilfree said. "And the photograph."

"Got any ideas, Pilfree?"

"In that void of a skull?" Bobbie Leigh said, tapping Pilfree's head with her knuckles.

"Get away from me!"

"Teamwork, y'all. Remember?"

"Sorry, doofus," Bobbie Leigh said. "I stand ready for your ideas."

Pilfree brushed his palm across his hair. "I've seen this before." He studied the photograph, hoping some long-latent bell stashed deep within the recesses of his brain might ring.

"Watered wheel, sleeping in the depths," Taylor said.

"Sounds like a shipwreck to me," Bobbie Leigh blurted.

"Exactly!" Pilfree said. "Which explains its rusty, corroded appearance. But *what* shipwreck? And this whatever-it-is looks like *more than one* wheel."

"Do we have to solve all these challenges tonight?" Bobbie Leigh asked, yawning. "It's getting late, and I'm not thinking straight."

"What does "getting late" have to do with *you* not thinking straight?" Pilfree asked, shaking his head.

"What'd you say, Pil-boy?" Bobbie Leigh asked, rubbing her eyes. "Couldn't hear you over my yawning."

"Nothing, BL," Taylor said, taking the photo and poem from Pilfree and stuffing them and the wax-sealed envelope into her backpack. "You're right, BL. It is late. Let's sleep on this and meet tomorrow morning on my front porch, 8:00."

"*Eight* o'clock?" Bobbie Leigh said. "Sure you don't want to back that up to, say, *5:00*? I mean, who needs sleep!"

"Do we have to cross back over the river same as we got here?" Pilfree asked.

"We have the fourth challenge," Taylor answered. "I think we're safe to use the bridge going back."

"Just in case, we'll let Pilfree cross first," Bobbie Leigh said between yawns.

"Tell you what, BL," Taylor said, reconsidering meeting at her house in the morning, "let's each of us do our own research, from our own computers. Then, meet on my front porch at 2:00 tomorrow afternoon."

"Good," Bobbie Leigh whispered. "I can sleep in."

"If anyone believes they've stumbled across anything significant," Pilfree suggested, "call the others and share your thoughts.

"Summer camp's looking better all the time," Bobbie Leigh said as the trio made their way toward the bridge over Sagitaw River.

12

Wheel of Fortune

Taylor tapped her keyboard with one hand of fingers as she gulped milk from a glass held with the fingers of her other.

"Want more pancakes, Taylor?" Susan asked from downstairs. "Eggs, too, if you'll have them."

"No, thanks, Mom. I'm good."

"Dad and I are on our way to get groceries, maybe swing over to the Home Depot."

"Okay, Mom."

"Need anything?"

"No, Mom. I'm good."

Susan paused, unaccustomed to Taylor's succinct replies, not to mention her absence from the family table on a summer morning.

"Okay, then. See you after while. Miss Peasy apple pie in the fridge."

"Go, already," Taylor whispered, looking at the poem, her fingers poised to type a string of search words, "so I can concentrate." She recalled Bobbie Leigh's stumble into a possible direction toward solving this challenge: 'Sounds like a shipwreck to me' Taylor remembered her saying. She typed.

"Shipwreck. Wheel." Taylor pressed enter. "Well, here are plenty of images of ships' wheels but nothing that looks like this multi-wheeled picture left by Blythington. Ugh. Note to self: never name my kid 'Blythington'.

"So, let me add 'Greek' to this search. Okay, so what have we *here?*" she said, leaning forward in her chair, gazing upon a term she'd never before seen, aside an image she *had* seen—yesterday. A smile crossed her face.

Meanwhile, Pilfree took a bite from his morning poptart, set the remainder on a paper towel and pressed a button on his timer. His hands and fingers dashed back and forth. His eyes danced side to side, as if in an involuntary response to an electrical shock.

"Time!" he shouted, pressing the timer button. "*Twenty-three seconds?*" he said in disbelief, a palm slapping his forehead. "Man, I did better than that last *month!* I'll *never* break the record at this rate of *decline.*" Pilfree sighed, approaching his laptop. He shoved the timer into his desk drawer and a pocket watch into his pocket.

"Wonder if Taylor's come up with anything yet." He scratched his head and entered some search words. "No telling what this clue is all about. Wheels with teeth. Watered depths. Shipwrecks. *Hewlett-Packard* of its day? Yeah, *right.* Greece to ... what's *this?*" Pilfree stared wide-eyed at the screen. "*Yes!* By George, this is *it!*" He grabbed his smart phone and tapped in Taylor's quick-dial. "But what *is* it?"

"Hello?" Taylor answered.

"It's me. Pilfree!"

"I was just about to call you, Pilfree!" Taylor said. "I think I have something."

"Me, too! Does your 'something' start with the letter 'A'?"

"And *end* with the letter 'A'?" Taylor said, extending the question.

"Antikythera?" they said together.

"It's the Antikythera Mechanism!" Taylor shouted.

"Yes, it is!" Pilfree confirmed. "So, have you figured out what this mechanism is and what Challenge #4 has to do with it?"

"Should we call Bobbie Leigh?" Taylor asked.

"What, and wake her up? Nah."

"I read that the Antikythera Mechanism was the first known computer, designed to calculate eclipses of the moon and sun and to determine positions of the moon for a given future date," Taylor said.

Pilfree added, "It has twenty-seven wheeled gears, the total teeth of each having a relationship to a prime number, such as nineteen and twenty-three and—"

"—and so, do you think we've earned the right to read the message inside the red wax-sealed envelope?" Taylor asked.

"I suppose ... yes, we have," Pilfree replied, nervously picking up his Rubik's Cube. "One way to know for sure."

"I know," Taylor acknowledged, staring at the envelope in her palm. "Well, let's not do it until Bobbie Leigh is with us. I'll call her." Taylor checked the time. "It's 9:38. Meet us at my house. Eleven o'clock."

"Will do."

Taylor pressed call-end and then the quick-dial for Bobbie Leigh. She waited. "*Wake up*, Bobbie Leigh, and answer the phone!"

"Talk to me!"

"Talk to me?" Taylor responded.

"Yeah, talk to me, whoever you are."

"BL, this is *Taylor*. What if I'd been your mom or dad, or even the President of the United States?"

"*Are* you my mom or dad or the President of the United States?"

"Well ... no, but–"

"Then, it's 'talk to me'."

"Bobbie Leigh, are you awake?"

"Of *course*, I'm awake. Been awake since 6:30, busy researching our little clue."

"Wow," Taylor answered in stunned surprise. "Okay, then. Well, so have I. Pilfree, too. And I think we've figured this thing out."

Bobbie Leigh took a sip of her orange juice. "Me, too," she said as cavalierly as if she'd acknowledged having a heartbeat.

"What? You, too?"

"It was *simple*, just like *all* of BJW's clues so far have turned out to be, especially simple since *I* was the teammate who suggested the shipwreck idea."

"Indeed you did. And your answer?"

"The Antikythera Mechanism, of course," Bobbie Leigh replied, followed by a yawn, followed by a slurp from her orange juice straw. "I even watched a video about it."

Taylor said nothing for several seconds.

"Are you there?" Bobbie Leigh asked, tapping on her phone.

"I'm here," Taylor replied. "Just trying to decide if I pressed the right speed dial, if I called the right person, is all."

"Funny, *ha, ha!* Don't go Pilfree on me, Taylor."

"So, we're meeting at my house at 11:00, to open the envelope. Be here, smarty pants."

"You just make sure you don't open it any sooner, Taylor Smart!"

The poem clue, it turned out, was not so daunting after all, as far as its actual resolution was concerned. The scythe of technology had cut swiftly through the chaff of their searches. What, the three thought, had such an ancient device as the Antikythera Mechanism to do with what surely must be the *real* challenge contained within the waiting wax-sealed envelope?

Pilfree arrived at the front porch fifteen minutes early, having walked the two-mile distance from his home to Taylor's while in constant practice with his Rubik's Cube, not once looking up from it, adroitly avoiding death by vehicle as he crossed streets, as if relying solely on an auto-pilot sixth sense.

"I'm here!" Pilfree shouted. Without pause, he let loose another announcement, "I'm *here*. Taylor Sm—"

"I *know* you're here, Pilfree," Taylor interrupted from her raised bedroom window. "The whole *neighborhood* knows you're here!"

"Sorry, Taylor. Where's Bobbie Leigh?"

"I'll be right down," Taylor said.

"I'll be right here," he replied.

Taylor opened the front door, glass of milk in hand. "Not only are you here, you're here *early*."

Pilfree pulled out his pocket watch. "So I am."

"You can solve Rubik's Cubes in a matter of *seconds*, but you rely on a *pocket watch* for time? I thought you were the human sundial."

"A 1906 Hamilton Railroad pocket watch, to be exact," Pilfree replied, holding the watch high and smiling broadly. "Twenty-one jewels and not a second slow. This thing'd give atomic clocks a run for their money. Marvels of time-keeping ingenuity, these babies. Belonged to my grandfather-plus-two."

"What's a grandfather-*plus-two*?"

"Great-great grandfather."

"Why didn't you just *say* great-great grandfather, you doofus!" shouted Bobbie Leigh, skidding to a pebble-slinging stop on her bike.

Pilfree returned the watch to the pocket of his plaid red-yellow-and-blue pants. "I was sort of hoping *you* had slept in this morning."

"You're not *that* lucky, Pil-boy," Bobbie Leigh said. "Besides, I've got this poem thing figured out. Have *you?*"

"Matter of fact, I have. Taylor, too, I believe. Why don't you tell us the answer ... BL."

"See what you've done, Taylor?" Bobbie Leigh protested. "Now the Pil-boy's latched onto it."

"One veggie short of a sandwich," Pilfree said, laughing.

"I'm gonna toss that cube of yours into the street!" Bobbie Leigh shouted, "and let some car crush it. And, for your information, the tomato is a *fruit*, not a veggie. By the way, the answer is the Antikythera Mechanism."

"Maybe *you're* the fruit? A *coconut!*"

"Bobbie Leigh's pretty smart, Pilfree," Taylor observed.

"Gotta hand it to the little sandwich," Pilfree admitted. Bobbie Leigh reached for the Rubik's Cube. Pilfree jerked back his hand. "Seriously, Bobbie Leigh, well done."

"So, where's the envelope?" Bobbie Leigh asked.

"Right here," Taylor replied, pulling the folded document from her jeans pocket. "Still sealed, as promised."

"Open it," Pilfree said.

"That honor should go to Bobbie Leigh," Taylor said, handing the envelope to her.

"As well it should!" Bobbie Leigh agreed.

Bobbie Leigh chiseled away the red wax with her thumb nail. "Here goes," she said, lifting the flap and pulling the vellum document from its hold.

She handed the document to Taylor, who, squinting, attempted to make sense of the ornate calligraphy. Taylor shifted her glasses from the top of her head to the front of her eyes.

"I just noticed," Bobbie Leigh said. "You wear *glasses?* Since when?"

"Since when I can't see *without* them, especially up close," Taylor answered. "Okay, here it is: 'If you are reading this, you have satisfied the requirements of Challenge #4, Part A. Congratulations.

"'As you now know, the Antikythera Mechanism, named for the Greek island near which the ship carrying the device sank, is considered the world's first known computer and was used to predict lunar and solar eclipses. Which brings us to Part B and the essence of the Game.'"

"*Essence* of the game?" Pilfree repeated.

"Don't interrupt, Pilfree!" Bobbie Leigh said. "Keep reading, Taylor."

"'As a test of your level of commitment to the challenges of life, and to the well-being of each other, one of you will be taken hostage and will be delivered to a site not known to the remaining two of you until you are revealed such in Challenge #5.'"

Taylor lowered the document to her lap and looked at her friends. Eyes met, all filled with questions and doubts.

"That's *it?*" Pilfree asked.

"So, wait a minute," Bobbie Leigh said. "What's any of *this* have to do with the Antikythera Mechanism?"

"Obviously, BJW is not revealing that to us yet," Pilfree replied. "Besides, my interest has now shifted from that to this hostage revelation. What's *that* all about?"

"One of us will be taken hostage?" Bobbie Leigh said, stating the obvious. "No offense, guys, but I hope it ain't *me!*"

"I hope it's not you either," Pilfree said.

"Why, thank you, Pilfree."

"Because I'd be less inclined to try to find *you*."

Bobbie Leigh pulled her fist back with intent to deliver it into Pilfree's arm. Taylor hooked her arm around Bobbie Leigh's, stopping her forward thrust.

"If we *resist* being taken hostage, by whomever and whenever, we violate the rules of the game," Taylor noted, "and are thus subject to its consequences. Remember, no harm will come to us if we follow the directions of the challenges. He's testing our *strengths* ... *and* our weaknesses ... fears, too. Don't let him win."

"You're right, of course," Bobbie Leigh admitted, bringing her fist to her pocket. "Still want to *pop* you one, Pil-boy."

"Speaking of pop, this calls for a *frosted* poptart," Pilfree said, digging into his omnipresent box. "Might be my last."

13

Now It's Personal

"You don't think he'll try to take one of us in broad *daylight*, do you?" Bobbie Leigh asked. "And if we *don't* resist, how will we know *for sure* the kidnapper is related to this game, that in our zeal to 'follow directions' we're really giving ourselves over to some random serial killer?"

"And how do we know that killing one of us isn't part of BJW's game?" Pilfree added.

"Good questions, all," Taylor replied, tucking the vellum document back into the envelope and the envelope into her pocket. "I have questions of my own, including the ones you've asked. Fears, too. But we have to have faith, and lots of it."

"You said it, girl!"

"So, I guess there's nothing left to do but wait," Pilfree observed.

"At this point, no," replied Taylor, scanning the 360 degrees of their surroundings and wondering if faith was a commodity she could muster. "Let's talk about something else."

"What else is there to talk *about?*" Pilfree asked.

"When's the Rubik's Cube contest, Pilfree," Bobbie Leigh asked.

"This Friday," Pilfree answered, taking his cube from his backpack.

"What's the official land-speed record for solving a Rubik's Cube, anyhow, flame-fingers?"

"*Flame-fingers?*" Taylor said, smiling.

"Hey, I kinda like that, Bobbie Leigh!" Pilfree said. "Flame-fingers."

"So, what's the record?"

"There are lots of Rubik's Cube records," Pilfree replied, "because there are different cube sizes, such as this one, a

4x4x4. Records are held for 3x3x3, 5x5x5, even 7x7x7, and different scenarios for each size in each competition."

"Different scenarios?" Taylor asked.

"For example, solving the cube blindfolded, or with one's *feet*."

"With one's *feet?*" Bobbie Leigh asked. "I suppose they also have a category for solving the cube telekinetically?"

"That's coming, I'm sure," Pilfree answered.

"So, what are the specifics of your competition this Friday?" Taylor asked.

"It's an official, sanctioned event," Pilfree replied with a sigh.

"Why so downtrodden?" Taylor asked. "I thought these sorts of things for you were ... well, like eating poptarts."

"The standing record for this event is 7.26 seconds. So far, I've not been able to beat 9.47 seconds. The difference might as well be eternity!"

"Let me see that thing," Bobbie Leigh said, taking it from Pilfree's hand. "Looks easy enough."

"I've tried it, Bobbie Leigh," Taylor said. "It's like trying to talk your parents into letting you go on unchaperoned dates."

"Like I said, looks easy."

"Well it's not," Pilfree said, frustrated, grabbing the cube from Bobbie Leigh. "First prize is two-hundred fifty dollars and a trophy, not to mention the pride of victory."

"You can do it, Pilfree," Taylor said, hand on Pilfree's shoulder. "We have confidence in you."

"Unless *you're* the one kidnapped," Bobbie Leigh added.

"There *is* that," Pilfree said.

"I need to go," Taylor said. "Mom wants me to vacuum the house while she and Dad do yard work."

"Can't that wait, Taylor," Bobbie Leigh asked.

"That's what I said to Mom. She said my allowance could wait, too."

"Bummer," Pilfree said as he zipped through another Rubik's exercise. "Well, watch your backs, you two."

"Let's agree that both of you will call or text me at six o'clock each evening, to check in," Taylor suggested.

"Agreed," came the simultaneous reply.

"Wait," Bobbie Leigh said.

"What, BL?"

"Okay, so what if one of us *is* kidnapped. And I presume the other two will think a kidnapping has occurred when each of us doesn't check in. Then what? What'll we do? Where will we go to look?"

"My guess is BJW's already thought of that," Taylor replied, "and will let the other two know how to proceed. Until that time, we wait. But don't mention any of this to your parents. Not a *word!*"

"I could tell my parents the whole story," Bobbie Leigh said, reaching for Pilfree's box of poptarts, "in living color detail, and they'd never hear a word I uttered."

"As for me," Pilfree said, "no time for telling. It's practice, practice, practice!"

"Remember, six o'clock. Sharp!" Taylor reminded them.

14

It's in the Bag

Five days passed. Each evening, the three checked in. So far, no kidnapper, no hostage. Friday had arrived, and now Pilfree's heart pounded like a boxer's fists upon the bag, as he awaited the Rubik's Cube contest. Bobbie Leigh stood near the lineup of ten contestants, each of whom had a waist-high card table in their front, atop of which rested one 4x4x4 Rubik's Cube arrayed in a jumble of color combinations. The ten cubes had been pre-set identically to ensure the equal footing of the competition. Pilfree saw Bobbie Leigh and gave a nervous wave of his hand.

"Where's Taylor?" he mouthed.

Bobbie Leigh looked side to side and behind her and shrugged her shoulders.

"Ladies and gentleman," one of the the contest proctors announced, "we will begin round one of this five-round Rubik's Cube regional championship in two minutes. To summarize, there will be a three-minute break between rounds. The highest and lowest times will be discarded, with the average time of the remaining three rounds used to determine each contestant's official time. Good luck to each of you."

Pilfree took a handkerchief from his pocket and dried the stress-produced clamminess from his palms. "So, where *is* she?" he repeated.

"She'll *be* here; don't worry!" Bobbie Leigh replied, doubting her own words as she scanned the area.

"At the sound of the bell, contestants...," the proctor announced.

DING!

The ten contestants frantically turned the four levels of their cubes, almost cartoonish in their speeds. ***BAM!*** One of the contestants, three persons to Pilfree's left, slammed down her cube to the table top.

The other contestants continued until their cubes were solved and then placed their completed cubes onto their tables for the recording of their times.

The proctor inspected the girl's cube assuring all its colors were appropriately aligned.

He held the cube high in the palm of his up-stretched arm. "Eight point three six seconds!" he shouted. The crowd issued its applause.

Each of the contestants' times were displayed in lights on big-screen monitors, and the first three-minute break ensued.

"So, you'll do better next time, Pilfree," Bobbie Leigh said, patting his arm.

"I don't know, BL. My time was ten point six seven. I'm still over two seconds off the pace."

"Gotta focus, flame-fingers!"

"Don't you think I *am* focused, Bobbie Leigh?"

"I think you're worried about Taylor," Bobbie Leigh said, searching the area with her eyes. "So am I, now that I mention it."

"You ... you think ..."

"I don't want to think about that, Pilfree," Bobbie Leigh answered. "Here, drink this." She handed Pilfree a bottle of water.

"Contestants, take your places," a proctor said.

"Here," Pilfree said, handing Bobbie Leigh the water bottle, tilted so that it splashed onto her arm and shirt.

"Gee, thanks!" Bobbie Leigh wiped her arm with her shirt. "Good luck to you, doofus!"

DING!

Two more rounds passed. Pilfree's times improved to the point that he won round three, by a half second. As he approached his table for round four, still two minutes away, he noticed a manila folder, its entire length, as well as its top and bottom widths, sealed with red wax, the folder itself wrapped with three rubber bands, nestled under his cube. Curious, he noticed no other contestants had a similar manila envelope on their tables, under their cubes. He took the folder and held it up for Bobbie Leigh to see.

"Did you put this here?" he mouthed.

"Not me," she mouthed in reply.

"*See* anyone put this here?"

"Just *open* it, Pilfree!"

Opening it, he found a sealed plastic freezer bag containing a semicircular iron object corroded with green and brown oxidation except for what appeared to Pilfree to be a brushed section in its middle. Pilfree raised and lowered the plastic bag, trying to get some idea of the object's weight, perhaps a pound, he thought. A paper fell from the folder to the table. Pilfree opened its folds and read silently:

> "By now you no doubt are concerned for the well-being of your teammate. That is a concern well-placed, for I do have her. Welcome to Challenge #5. This challenge is exclusively yours, dear reader. Yes, yours, for only you are in a position to conquer it. Meanwhile, hold tight to the object I have placed within the plastic bag. This iron object is not just priceless in the context of ancient artifacts. While not needed for Challenge 5, it

> is the KEY to your team's successful completion of this game. Do NOT misplace it.
>
> "So, what is Challenge #5, you ask? Simply this: you must win this Rubik's Cube contest. Win it, or ... lose it. Make certain it is not the latter."

"Places, contestants!" the proctor shouted. "Round four is about to begin!"

"What's the note say, Pilfree?" Bobbie Leigh asked. "And what's in the bag?"

Pilfree stared at Bobbie Leigh, eyes as big a silver dollars. He handed her the note and swallowed a throat full of half-dried saliva.

Bobbie Leigh read the note. She looked up at Pilfree just as round four started.

"Who *is* this person!" Bobbie Leigh whispered. "How does he know our *every* move, in *advance* of our every move?"

Just as Bobbie Leigh finished her last word, Pilfree slammed down his cube, taking round four with a time of five point seven seven seconds. His closest competitor finished a full three seconds slower. Round five awaited.

"Bobbie Leigh, I don't know if I can *do* this," Pilfree said, breathing fast and hard, as if he'd completed a sprint.

"Pilfree, you don't have a choice!" Bobbie Leigh said.

"But, they'll drop that time."

"They'll also drop your *worst* time, Pilfree," Bobbie Leigh reminded him. "Everyone's playing with the same rules here. For now, *focus!*"

Pilfree stared into Bobbie Leigh's eyes. He knew she was right. Looking at the updated cumulative results glaring brightly on the wallboard of monitors behind the tables, contestant six—Pilfree—held second place by fifteen hundredths of a second heading into the decisive round. Round five would have to be his personal best, not for merely winning the championship, but for preserving his and his friends' lives.

"Contestants! Places, please!"

"Bobbie Leigh—"

"You can *do* this, Pilfree," Bobbie Leigh said, squeezing Pilfree's forearm. "Rules of the game. The *will* of focus."

"He's taken Taylor, hasn't he? *She's* the hostage."

Bobbie Leigh believed so. The note said as much. "Don't worry about Taylor," she said. "Her mom's probably making her cut the grass or something."

Pilfree gave Bobbie Leigh a smirk of skepticism as he took his place for the last time behind his table. The differential between all contestants, first place to tenth place, was point seven one seconds, the tightest Rubik's Cube contest in the region's history. The ten contestants, save one, stood arrow straight, heads titled downward, as if in silent prayer or contemplation. Pilfree stared straight ahead, brows furrowed, determination building, anxious to see this through, to get this done, to win by the rules.

DING!

In the time it takes a resting heart to expend three beats, Pilfree slammed his cube to the table and expelled an audible sigh.

Huddled, two proctors inspected his cube to make sure all colors were properly aligned and that all rows were straight. Three point eight two seconds, a regional record, a world record for the 4x4x4 cube, and a time he knew would be dropped per the rules of determining official times.

Pilfree and Bobbie Leigh, along with scores of others, all gazes fixed upon the scoreboard, waited for the final official times to be posted. Seconds felt like hours. Bobbie Leigh clutched Pilfree's arm.

Then, like a blast from a July firework, Pilfree's name flashed large and bright at the top of the list of contestants.

Number one.

Official average time of six point four nine seconds. Pilfree's mouth opened, head tilted high, his broad teeth-sparkling smile expanding, as his lungs pushed a gush of air outward.

"You *did* it!" Bobbie Leigh shouted as she jerked Pilfree's arm up and down. "You're still a doofus, of course, but you *did* it!" Bobbie Leigh smiled, and Pilfree knew her insult was meant this time more as celebratory respect than a hurtful jab.

"Yes!" was all Pilfree could add. That, and a bite from a frosted poptart.

"So," Bobbie Leigh said, pointing with a tilt of her head, "What's in the bag?"

15

Fragment 83

"The bag?" Pilfree said. "Oh, the *plastic* bag!"

"Yes, the *plastic* bag!" Bobbie Leigh said. "I don't see any *other* bag."

Pilfree took the sealed bag and handed it to Bobbie Leigh. "Want to do the honors?"

Bobbie Leigh took the bag. "Wow! This thing's heavy. Why does he seal everything with *red wax*," she asked as she pulled apart the zip-lock seal, pieces of red wax crumbling to the ground and into the bag. "Seems sort of redundant in this case."

"Nice word, 'redundant'," Pilfree noted. "The wax is his trademark, I suppose."

“Thought you'd like that word. Learned it from Taylor.”

“Speaking of whom ... *now* what?” Pilfree asked.

Bobbie Leigh reached into the bag and pulled out the object. With it came another envelope, sealed, as they had come to expect, with red wax. Handing Pilfree the object, Bobbie Leigh broke the envelope's seal, taking the inside paper outside. She read aloud:

> “Congratulations! The fact that you are reading this note is proof you are still in my game, alive, and have won the Rubik's Cube contest, rising to the level of your skills despite your severest doubts, and thus are ready for the next Challenge, #6.
>
> “Of course, you are wondering about your missing friend. As I stated earlier, I do have her, safe, sound, and secure. But that won't always be the case, and not of my doing, you see, especially not if you fail in your interpretation of Challenge #6.

“Read the following poem. Contained therein are clues to your friend's whereabouts.

“Disregard for now—but do not discard—the iron object, what I term as Fragment 83. You will need it for the completion of a later challenge.

“As they say, good luck. But do not rely upon luck. Rely, instead, upon each other and your individual strengths, as you have thus far demonstrated. Luck is the crutch of the weak, the defense of last resort.

“Now, this challenge's clue to the location of your teammate.

“Deep within the darkened dank,
stone as smooth as silk,
hanging stems of yellow rock

and points as white as milk.

"Kinetic power flowing fast
that plummets at the brink,
pinned against a wall as sheer
as thoughts that cannot think.

"Take the combo that will free
the padlock 'round her blood;
you only have just half a day
before there flows the flood."

"What in the name of mac and cheese is he *talking* about, Bobbie Leigh?"

"That's why it's a challenge, Pilfree," Bobbie Leigh said, peeling away a rectangular two-inch-by one-inch strip of paper taped to the clue's paper. "We have to *figure out* what he's talking about. This must be the combination he referred to." Bobbie Leigh handed Pilfree the strip. "Memorize it first, then put it in your pocket."

"Why memorize it if I have it in my pocket?"

"I don't know, doofus! It sounds like something Taylor would ask you to do, so just *do* it, okay?"

"Okay, *okay*. 25 right," Pilfree read, "16 left; 32 right. 25 ... 16 ... 32. Got it." Pilfree wadded the paper and brought it toward his mouth, touching his lips.

"Don't *eat* it, you doofus!" Bobbie Leigh screamed. "It's *not* a poptart!"

"Oops. Sorry." Pilfree shoved the wadded paper into his pocket. "Too many Gilligan reruns."

"Geesh, Pilfree, how can you ace something so perplexing as a Rubik's Cube, yet defy even the most commonsensical things!"

"Me being me?" Pilfree answered with a question, now doubting its value as an excuse. "So, what do you make of this poem clue?"

"Other than his penchant for poetry, wonder what he means by 'flood'," Bobbie Leigh said, looking skyward. "River's low. Ain't a cloud in sight."

"Broken water main, maybe?" Pilfree speculated. "You don't suppose she's trapped somewhere in the sewer system."

"Yuck, Pilfree! No! *Think!*"

"This is one *creepy* clue," Pilfree said. 'Darkened dank'. 'Thoughts that cannot think'. 'Padlock 'round her *blood*'. That one's *really* creepy. Wonder what 'plummets at the brink' is all about?"

"Let's focus on one thing at a time," Bobbie Leigh suggested.

"You're sounding a lot like Taylor."

"Just picking up the slack. Okay, what do you think of when you see or hear the word 'brink', for example?"

"I dunno." Pilfree broke off a piece of poptart, scratching his forehead with it. "An armored car company?"

"That would be *Brinks*, Pil-boy."

"So, what do *you* think of, then?" Pilfree asked.

"Well, the first thought that comes to mind is a waterfall. You like examples, so here's one: 'I'm standing at the *brink* of this waterfall', or, 'don't get too close to the *brink*.'"

"Or," Pilfree offered, smiling, "how about 'how many times per minute does the average human eye brink?'"

"You really have issues, Pilfree," Bobbie Leigh said, sighing. "*Focus!*"

"I *am* focused. In moments such as this, a bit of humor never hurts."

"But where in Raventon ...". Bobbie Leigh stopped, her incomplete sentence suspended like a frozen rope.

"*What*, Bobbie Leigh!"

"The only waterfall in Raventon that has any *semblance* of a brink would be-e-e-e-e ..." she said, stringing out the last word as if to paste the thought to Pilfree's brain, hoping it would stick.

"*Sagitaw Falls!*" they shouted together.

"And the darkened dank *has* to be the Chamber of Skulls!" Bobbie Leigh shouted, excited.

"Chamber of *what?*"

"Never mind! Let's go!"

"Hey, kid, don't you want your Cube trophy?" a voice shouted from behind. "And don't forget your prize money! Excellent contest, by the way. Well done!"

"Keep it for now," Pilfree answered, slipping his backpack over his shoulder. "I'll be back to get it."

"Then you'll need this," the contest official replied, arm extended with the claim check in hand. "Present it to collect your trophy and money, unless you want your money now."

Pilfree took the slip of paper. "Thank you, sir," he said, looking at it, stuffing it into his pocket. A strange thought came over him, one he felt compelled to utter. "Somehow I don't think I'll be *needing* the money."

"Don't lose the claim check, son," the contest official said. Don't want such a stellar performance to go unrewarded."

"It's in a safe place," Pilfree replied. "How long is the claim check good?"

"A week. After that, the prize is forfeited to the second-place finisher."

"Go ahead and give the prize money to the second-place finisher," Pilfree blurted, his voice cracking, as if such a remark had not been his own.

"Where's that iron object, Pilfree?" Bobbie Leigh asked. "We can't lose–"

"*What* did I just tell that official?"

"Forget the contest, Pilfree," Bobbie Leigh said. Do you have that iron thingy?"

Pilfree patted his backpack. "Safe and sound, my dear."

"My *dear*?" Bobbie Leigh whispered out of sight and sound as she mounted her bike. She raised one eyebrow and smiled.

"Bobbie Leigh!" Pilfree shouted.

"What!"

"Look."

Swirling gray-green clouds appeared in the northwestern sky above the wind-swayed trees.

You only have just half a day before there comes a flood, Bobbie Leigh thought, remembering the poem as she took in the sight of storm clouds gathering. "How does BJW *know* these things?"

16

At the Brink

Lightning sliced the noon sky, thunder following seconds after. Gusts of wind pushed and pulled the trees. Scattered balls of rain exploded against the dirt road's dust, carving mini-craters and predicting the fury to come. Pilfree and Bobbie Leigh slid their bikes to a halt at the entrance to the Chamber of Skulls.

"C'mon, Pilfree!" Bobbie Leigh said.

"So *this* is the famous cave where it all happened," Pilfree said, scanning the area as might a tourist.

"This is the Chamber of Skulls, all right."

"You really think Taylor's in *there?*"

"I don't *think* she is," Bobbie Leigh replied. "I *know she is*!" As they entered the cave, torrents of rain swept the outside world, its mist swirling in the cave entrance.

"Wow! We *barely* beat that storm."

"Best keep your mind on the storm ahead, Pilfree. Not claustrophobic, are you?"

"Only in confined spaces."

"This is the source of the flood BJW was talking about," Bobbie Leigh said. "Sagitaw River flows through this cave. Any storm's going to produce a flash flood."

"But how does he *know* all these things, that they're going to happen, I mean?" Pilfree asked. "He's like some clairvoyant, a Nostradamus. How did he *know* I would enter a Rubik's Cube contest ... and *win*! *How*, Bobbie Leigh, did he know there would be *three* of us playing this crazy game of his? He always seems to be a step ahead of us."

"I'm just glad your questions are *not* among the challenges we have to conquer, Pilfree, challenges we would have to solve in order to survive."

Pilfree stared in to Bobbie Leigh's eyes. "How do we know they *won't be?*"

Bobbie Leigh stood silent, not willing to ponder an answer to Pilfree's last question.

"Let's go, Pilfree," Bobbie Leigh said, taking out her flashlight and scoping the shadowed spaces ahead, trying to locate the narrow tunnel opening through which they would have to crawl, through which she and Taylor had crawled a year before.

"There it is, Pilfree!" Bobbie Leigh shouted.

"There *what* is?"

"Just follow me!"

Pilfree followed Bobbie Leigh's trot, flashlight light bobbing from point to point. She stopped.

"Hold this," Bobbie Leigh said, handing Pilfree the flashlight. "This is a tight crawl, Pilfree, so try to keep the light shining over my head, ahead of me, so I can see. Watch for stalactites, and prepare yourself for one *claustrophobic crawl.*"

"What a *great* cave!" Pilfree observed.

"You ain't seen *nothin'* yet ... my dear."

The tunnel, roughly two feet by three feet at its widest and tallest, meandered left and right, like crawling through the length of a giant snake. Dampness soaked their jeans at the knees, the moisture spreading above and below those contact points, chilling their goose-bumped skin to the bones.

"Just how long is–***OW!***–this tunnel, Bobbie Leigh?"

"Hit your head, did you?"

Pilfree rubbed his fingertips across the wound. "Enough to bleed, too."

"It'll stop," Bobbie Leigh said. "Let's go."

"I feel like I'm on hallowed ground, knowing what you and Taylor went through," Pilfree said, assessing the severity of his head wound.

"Stay with me, Pilfree. And keep the light high!"

After several minutes, the pair emerged into the expanse of the great 100-feet-tall chamber, its ancient columns of flowstone towering from floor to ceiling, and, glistening in their flashlight-polished glow, a forest of stalactites and stalagmites guarding every direction. Pilfree stared, wondering how all his life he had missed knowing of this wonder of nature practically in his backyard.

"Snap out of it, Pilfree!" Bobbie Leigh shouted, her voice tumbling from wall to wall. She pointed. "We have Taylor to fetch! Through *there.*"

"*Assuming* she's there."

"Trust me, she's there!"

"So, how do we get from here to there, to Taylor?"

"All you have to do, my dear, is shut up and follow me," Bobbie Leigh instructed. "Now give me that flashlight."

"Wow!" Pilfree managed, struggling to find the appropriate descriptive words. "It's ... it's so *dark* in here," he said, looking behind him, opposite the direction of the flashlight.

"I'm sure the new regional Rubik's Cube champion can come up with the *reason* for that."

"Well, actually," Pilfree said, stopping to survey the area they had trekked, "there is no such thing as darkness; just the *absence of light*. And since sunlight has no access to this part of the cave ... Hey! Where'd you go! *Bobbie Leigh!*"

"It's always semantics with you," said Bobbie Leigh, flipping the flashlight's switch. "*Lighten up*, Pilfree! Hey, I made a joke! Get it? *Lighten* up."

Pilfree rubbed his wounded head.

A muffled lull grew to an audible rush as they made their way through a narrow passage between house-sized boulders. The sound, at first like that of the distant roar of a jet plane, grew louder with each step until the sound reached a near equivalent of standing on the tarmac *with* that jet plane. Bobbie Leigh stopped, her right hand raised. Pilfree froze, wiping away aggravating spits of water falling onto his face.

"Pilfree, this is where things get dangerous," Bobbie Leigh said as she shone her flashlight to their two-o'clock. Thirty feet ahead, the roar became water, an underground river of raging white, slapping cave boulders, taking in the torrent of storm runoff from the slopes that rose above the cave. Waves of water exploded against the walls as the river's path bent.

"Oh my God!" Pilfree shouted as the light revealed the power before him. Kinetic power, just as the clue had suggested. Trying to steady his fear of the sight before him, Pilfree stumbled backwards through the mistiness of the cave air.

"Calm down, Pil-boy," Bobbie Leigh shouted with a measure of lilting assurance, if not lighthearted derision, just enough to keep Pilfree from bolting with abject fear into the abyss of darkness.

"That stream turns into Sagitaw Falls, about fifty feet ahead, around another bend. Takes a real ninety-degree turn, three-dimensionally speaking, if you get my drift. The falls is the real roar you're hearing, and that, my dear, is where we'll find Taylor."

"Sag ... Sagitaw Falls?"

"All four hundred-something feet of it," Bobbie Leigh confirmed.

"Taylor!" Pilfree shouted, hands cupped around his mouth. "Taylor, can you *hear* me?"

"Pilfree, she can't hear you! I can *barely* hear you! Water's too loud! Let's move!"

Pilfree and Bobbie Leigh toed the narrow strip of relatively dry ground, an alternating surface of mud and stone, the instincts of their left hands futilely probing and grasping the flat, polished surfaces of the knobby rock wall. The stream grew louder, more intense in its volume, as it channeled the storm's runoff, the flood that challenge #6 spoke of. Each step took the pair closer to the water's edge, as if drawing them into its mesmerizing rush.

Then, a gust of bright air met them as they squeezed their final turn between sheets of flowstone and a raging river. A gaping cavity through the side of the mountain, large enough to plug with the Hindenburg, provided the exit for the cave stream, its water swirling wildly, pounding left and right against anything in its way, as it swept over and straight down with breathtaking abruptness the ninety-degree turn to which Bobbie Leigh had alluded.

“How far down did you say was the drop?” Pilfree shouted.

“Does it really matter?” Bobbie Leigh replied. “Let's just say you'd be late for dinner!”

“*Now* what!” Pilfree said.

“We have to get out on that ledge. That's where Taylor'll be,” Bobbie Leigh said, “I can promise you that. Get the lock combo ready!”

“Hey, what's this?” Pilfree asked, pointing to a clump against the wall beside the water's exit. Bobbie Leigh looked.

"That ... that's my *backpack*, from that *other* adventure, last year," she said. "Left it here and forgot all about it! Don't let me forget to take it when we leave. There's a spear point in it; found it right here in this cave."

"Don't you mean *projectile* point?"

"Oh, look!" Bobbie Leigh said, pointing her flashlight straight into Pilfree's eyes. "I've found *Taylor!*"

"What are you talking–"

"Arrowhead, projectile point," Bobbie Leigh said, frustrated, "what *difference* does it make!"

"I take it Taylor has made the distinction clear *to* you," Pilfree said, "and it didn't sit too well *with* you."

Bobbie Leigh sighed. *My dear, indeed,* she thought, shaking her head. She stepped through a curtain of water cascading from somewhere within the blackened ceiling above. Bolts of ice-cold, gasp-inducing water burst upon her head, shoulders, and arms. She reached for the cave wall at the opening, pulling herself forward to the brink of the outside world–just two feet shy of the edge of the raging flow of Sagitaw Falls. Looking left, water sliding down her face, she smiled.

"I thought you two would *never* find me!" Taylor shouted.

"He has you locked to *iron stakes?*" Pilfree observed.

"Hope you have the key," Taylor said.

"Pil-boy's got it," Bobbie Leigh answered.

"I don't have the key, but I *do* have the combination, right ... right ... um."

Pilfree pillaged his pockets, pulling out two wadded dollars and the claim check for his Rubik's Cube contest prize, plus half a soggy poptart, a wheatback penny, and a chess pawn. "Ah, *here* it is!"

"So where's your chess board, Pilfree?" Bobbie Leigh mocked.

"In my brain, my dear."

"How'd you two know where to find me?" Taylor asked.

"Another one of BJW's literary masterpieces, how else?" Bobbie Leigh replied.

"Should've known."

"Better question is," Bobbie Leigh asked, "how were you captured and brought here?"

"I ... I don't remember. The only thing I *do* remember is going to bed last night, thinking about Pilfree's Rubik's Cube contest."

"Which, by the way, I *won!*" Pilfree said, thumbs anchored to his suspenders.

"As I knew you would," Taylor replied. "Next thing I know, I feel water splashing my face, only to discover I'm locked to these two iron bars at the brink of Sagitaw Falls. Speaking of which, *unlock me!*"

"He must have come into your room, drugged you somehow, and taken you here," Bobbie Leigh speculated.

"Mom and Dad must be freaking out by now," Taylor said as she watched the thundering water plunge over the brink. She wiped water droplets from her eyes. "Okay, Pilfree, get me out of here."

"I ... um ... I *would*, except ..."

"Except ... *what?*" Bobbie Leigh said, a wave of realization falling over her.

"Except that the piece of paper it was written on just sailed from my fingers and down that way," Pilfree said, pointing toward the water of Sagitaw Falls.

"You *dolt!*" shouted Bobbie Leigh.

"Not to worry, my dear," Pilfree replied, pointing to his head. "In my brain."

"Not to *worry?* Just how are we going to free Taylor?"

"A little thing called memory, *that's* how."

"Ah, yes," Bobbie Leigh remembered, "you *memorized* the combination!"

"Per your instructions."

"Good boy!"

"You know," Pilfree observed, as he momentarily forgot the tumult of the falls and the plight of his friend, "this is quite a view of the valley. Fields and farms, laid out like patches on one of my grandmama's quilts–"

"Pilfree!" the girls shouted.

"The combination ... yeah ...," he said, "I think I've got it. Let's see ... 25 right; 14 left ... 32 right." He smiled. "No, *wait!*"

"What!"

"*16* left."

17

Its Weight in Gold

"This's no good anymore," Bobbie Leigh said, lifting up the year-old abandoned backpack with her thumb and forefinger. "It's all moldy and wet. Stinks, too."

"Don't *leave* it here," Taylor said.

"Why not? It's been here over a year."

"Because it's like littering, that's why not," Pilfree replied.

"Okay, so I'll toss it." Bobbie Leigh swung her arm back, ready to heave the pack over the falls and into its four-hundred-plus foot plunge.

"*Wait!*" Taylor shouted.

"What!"

"Didn't you leave a projectile point in one of the pockets?"

"You mean an *arrowhead?*"

"Okay, yes, an arrowhead! See if it's there."

"I don't think ... wait ... well, what do you know, so I *did*!" Bobbie Leigh announced, lifting a four-inch white quartzite, side-notched knife point from the mildewed pocket. Pilfree reached for the ancient artifact.

"Told ya. Now, *don't* toss the pack," Taylor said.

"Why not? It's nothing more to me now, except excess baggage."

"Maybe there's one of your sandwiches still inside, you know, for Pilfree. He seems to like old things, too."

"Funny, Mewels," Bobbie Leigh said.

"Did somebody say 'sandwich'?"

"It's just a useless backpack and ... wait ... What's this?" Bobbie Leigh asked as her hand rummaged through the pockets for anything else worth salvaging.

"What's *what?*" Pilfree teased, "The sandwich?"

"There's *no sandwich*, Pil-boy!"

"So, what have you found?" Taylor asked.

"This," she said, slowly lifting an off-white envelope, its red-wax seal emblazoned with the initials of BJW.

"And you ... you were about to *toss* that pack down ... there," Pilfree said, swallowing hard as water thundered over the brink.

"I was, wasn't I," Bobbie Leigh admitted. "You ... you open it, Taylor."

"Okay," she agreed, breaching the wax seal and lifting the envelope's flap. "We ... we almost threw away Challenge #7."

The three looked silently at each other, aware that their careless attitude, after having come so far and accomplished so much, had nearly cost them the game, perhaps their lives.

"So ... um ... read it," Pilfree said, clearing his throat.

"You read it, Pilfree," Taylor replied, handing him the document.

"Okay." Pilfree swallowed, moistening his dry throat. "'This is where I expected you to fail, here at the falls, with the dismissal, even the discard, of Bobbie Leigh's weathered backpack. But you worked together, admonishing your teammate's carelessness by encouraging the recovery of a valuable artifact. Well done, indeed. Let's hope you are in possession of the other backpack, for within it resides another, more-valuable artifact, Fragment 83, worth far more than its weight in gold."

"The *other* backpack?" Taylor asked.

"*This* one," Pilfree said, pulling his own off his shoulders.

"What's he talking about, worth far more than its weight in gold?" Taylor asked.

"Fragment 83," Pilfree answered as he lifted the pound-plus object from his pack.

"Fragment 83? What's fragment—"

"Of the the Antikythera Mechanism," Bobbie Leigh replied. "Just look at it, all corroded and green and rusted, just like the photos of the AM we've seen online. What's the challenge say?"

Pilfree opened the vellum document, revealing the instructions of Challenge #7.

"Says, 'Take Fragment 83 from your backpack.'"

"Got it," Bobbie Leigh confirmed, holding it high. Why's it called Fragment 83?"

"Because," Taylor replied, "divers found eighty-two fragments of the Antikythera Mechanism. Either BJW somehow found number eighty-three, or this fragment's fictitious, something he created for purposes of his game."

Pilfree continued. "'As you can see, this fragment is as large as the main fragment itself and is inscribed with numerous symbols and lettering. But what do the symbols and lettering say? What is their message, and how is that message relevant to here and now, to this game, to you?

"'Your challenge is to discover the inscriptions' meanings, at least enough to reveal their world-changing message. It's a dirty job, but you have six days to dig up the solution. If your interpretations of the inscriptions' meanings are incorrect, or if you fail in carrying out their instructions, a seventh day will be irrelevant—to everyone, everywhere.'"

The three sat silent for a couple of minutes as the water of Sagitaw Falls roared over its brink to the waiting river below, as if symbolically carrying their futures with it.

"Anyone have ... any bright ideas?" Taylor asked.

"It's all Greek to me," Bobbie Leigh quipped.

"Looks real," Pilfree added. "Are you okay, Taylor?"

"Just tired. Can't seem to get my strength up lately," Taylor replied.

"Six days." Bobbie Leigh said. "*Then* what?"

"He says it's irrelevant," Pilfree replied.

"Why, the *end of the world*, of course," Bobbie Leigh added. "Let's just go home, eat ice cream until our brains freeze, and watch some TV. 'Cause there's *no way* we're gonna decipher *that!*"

"Oh, I don't know," Pilfree said, chin in palm.

"So, Pil-boy, you think you got this?"

"Maybe, Bobbie Leigh, and, like all his other challenges, the answer is probably right in front of us."

"How so?" Taylor inquired.

"Consider this," Pilfree said. "His own words in Challenge #7 infer some end-of-the-world scenario, after six days, unless we 'dig up' the solution. And who said anything about *deciphering?*"

"We *have* to decipher!" a frustrated Bobbie Leigh shouted. "How else–"

"So, Pilfree ...," Taylor interrupted.

"So, how would BJW *know* that, if he hadn't himself *already* deciphered the fragment's inscriptions?"

"The fragment probably has some sort of Nostradamus-like meaning, a prediction maybe, and BJW already *knows* what it is?" Taylor asked.

"All we have to do is figure out where he may have written down the message's meaning, because you *know* he's written it down. Else, we wouldn't have *thought* of it!" Pilfree said, a tooth-filled smile crossing his face.

"Man, we might as well decipher the inscriptions *ourselves*," Bobbie Leigh said. "Even if he *did* write it down, *finding* it is going to be like finding a needle in a silo filled with grain!"

"You mean a needle in a haystack, don't you?" Pilfree asked.

"You have your cliches; I have mine," Bobbie Leigh replied. "Besides, if only it were *that* easy, Pil-boy."

"Maybe it *is* that easy, *easier* even," Taylor said, excitement building in her voice. "BJW knows that the essence of these challenges does not reside in their *details*, or, as I like to call them, the weeds."

"Okay, *and* ..." Bobbie Leigh said.

"Deciphering the inscriptions is sort of a *sub*-challenge," Taylor explained. "The sub-challenges are made to appear difficult but are really just smokescreens, meant as diversions, perhaps, but also meant to be relatively easy to overcome. The *real* challenge is carrying out the message's instructions, using our wits and teamwork."

"Okay, *and* ...," Bobbie Leigh repeated.

"Don't you *see?*" Taylor begged.

"*I* do," Pilfree said.

"So, *tell me*, before I hurl myself over those falls!"

"Chill out, Bobbie Leigh. Curb your frustration and think about the challenge, the *words* BJW used. BJW told us the job would be "dirty" and that we'd have to "dig up" the solution."

"Okay, *and* ...."

"Bobbie Leigh, we're heading back to the *cemetery*. It's just a *hunch*, I know, but we're going to dig up BJW's ... grave," Taylor revealed.

"His *grave!*" Bobbie Leigh shouted.

"Maybe not his grave," Taylor said, "but where his grave would be ... according to his tombstone."

"So you think he's orchestrating this whole game, real-time, as we live and breathe?" Pilfree asked.

"I think he's watching our every move, even *now*," Taylor replied. "It's almost as if he were ... one of *us*."

18

The Blood Moon Decipher

The muted glows of neighborhood streetlights and low-wattage cemetery lights cast eerie shadows of headstones, dark polygons that stretched in all directions across the grounds.

"Where's Pilfree?" Bobbie Leigh asked, straining to discern dancing shadows of breeze-blown branches from silhouettes of living humans. "He's never on time for *anything!*"

"He'll *be* here; he's responsible for the shovel."

"This place creeps me out, especially on cloudy nights. And if we get *caught*–"

"We won't get caught, Bobbie Leigh," Taylor insisted. "A cloudy night actually benefits us. And keep your voice to a *whisper.*"

"So, what did your parents have to say about you not being home for breakfast after the night you were kidnapped?"

"Say?" Taylor responded. "Oh, nothing, really. They just sort of assumed I left the house early, skipped breakfast, you know, summer stuff."

"Sounds so *unlike* them, Taylor—"

"That y'all?" Pilfree shouted.

"So much for keeping it to a whisper," Bobbie Leigh said.

"Over here, Pilfree," Taylor directed. "And *hush up!*"

"Sorry I'm late," Pilfree said as he lifted the shovel. "Bet you thought I'd forget it, didn't you?"

"Start digging, Pil-boy."

"You make me sound like some *drug* dealer."

"*Aren't* you? You're certainly a *dope*. Now, dig!"

"And ruin these wonderful *new* checkered sneakers?" Pilfree said, chuckling. His attempt to brighten the macabre task before them instead drew stoic stares. "Okay, okay, I'm digging."

Pilfree sank the shovel into soil dampened by the recent rain. "Bobbie Leigh, keep the light shining *here*, please," he said.

After thirty minutes and a depth of two feet, Pilfree stopped. He wiped his forehead with his sleeve. "I ... I don't think anything's here, Taylor."

Taylor handed him a bottle of water. "Looks that way, I'm afraid."

"Well, *somebody's* been here," Bobbie Leigh noticed.

"How do you know that?" Pilfree asked.

"By all the Zippy Burger wrappers in that last shovel-full of dirt you tossed," she said, shining her flashlight upon the pile of mud. "Litterbugs!"

Pilfree and Taylor looked at each other. "Zippy Burger wrappers!" they shouted, immediately throwing their hands across their mouths, as if to contain the noise already escaped.

Pilfree dropped to his hands and knees, sifting aside chunks of mud and stone, revealing ten wads of wrappers. He selected one and smoothed out its waddedness over

Taylor's back. Handwritten in Old-English-style were the letters **Te.**'

"*Te?*" Bobbie Leigh said, "As in do-re-mi-fa-so-la- ... *te?* When did this game become a *musical?*"

"Look!" Taylor observed, "the number 5, top-left!"

Pilfree picked another wrapper and flattened its wrinkles. "It says '**Human to human**'. And look. Number 8, top-left. He's numbered the pieces."

"Are these *clues* to Fragment 83's meaning?" Bobbie Leigh asked.

"Not clues," Pilfree said. "The inscriptions' *translations!*"

"On *Zippy Burger* wrappers? How unromantic."

"I did sort of expect vellum, now that you mention it," Pilfree said.

"Okay, grab a wrapper and unwrinkle it as best you can," Taylor said. "Let's put the wrappers in numerical order. Then we'll know the inscription's message, or at least the message BJW wants us to have."

"I prefer Blythington," Pilfree said.

"You what?"

"Blythington. I prefer to call him Blythington. BJW sounds like a race car driver, or somebody's auto shop."

"You got something against auto racing and repair shops?" Taylor asked.

Pilfree noticed Taylor's tee shirt with its bold, leaning yellow *3*.

"Me? No, not really," Pilfree replied. "Just a personal preference is all."

"Keep your preferences to yourself," Bobbie Leigh said, "and get to straightening out these wrappers."

The ten wrappers were laid side by side, in numbered order. Taylor pointed the flashlight at the group of wrappers and read the completed message.

"'Shadow over moon; Sun to darkness; Moon to blood; Two of four moon shadows; Te; Trad; Plague released in city of blackbirds in tower of time; human to human; evil stopped, or death to all; Spread land to sea to land."

Pilfree took Fragment 83 from his backpack and surveyed the cryptic inscriptions. "*This* says ... *that?*"

"I'm guessing not, but the Antikythera Mechanism was a device able to predict solar and lunar eclipses, correct?"

Taylor asked. “Let's take this message line by line and pick out the key words.”

“Sounds like a plan,” Bobbie Leigh said. “'Shadow' and 'moon' look pretty key to me.”

“Okay, shadow and moon. Next wrapper.”

“'Sun' and 'darkness',” Pilfree said, “but that implies a solar eclipse. The first line is definitely referring to a *lunar* eclipse.”

“Keep going. I'm writing this down,” Taylor said.

“Wow, 'moon' again. And 'blood',” Bobbie Leigh said.

“Blood moon!” Pilfree blurted.

“Sounds scary,” Bobbie Leigh observed. “So ... what's a blood moon, anyway?”

“We just *had* one, this past February,” Taylor said.

“Are you talking about that really orange moon?” Bobbie Leigh asked.

“The very same,” Pilfree confirmed. “And we're due for another this month, August 7th, I believe.”

“That explains the next part, 'two of four moon shadows',” Taylor said. “First one was in February. Second one is this month.”

"Okay, so whatever it is this challenge requires must require it to be done during this next blood moon," Pilfree suggested.

"Sounds reasonable," Bobbie Leigh said, "but what about 'Te' and 'Trad'? Sound like a couple of hokie nicknames for boys!"

"Au contraire, my dear fellow-ette," Pilfree said.

"Tetrad," Taylor said, looking skyward.

"Exactly," Pilfree agreed.

"Exactly ... *what?*" said Bobbie Leigh. "Why am I *always* the last to get stuff around here!"

"Fate," Pilfree answered, "and genetics."

"Tetrad," Taylor said quickly, wanting to avoid another Bobbie Leigh-Pilfree face-off. "It's the astronomical term for lunar eclipses, specifically blood moons, which occur in groups of four, one eclipse every six months. *When* they occur, that is. They're pretty rare."

"Wow, Taylor, I'm impressed!" Pilfree said.

Bobbie Leigh folded her arms and gave Taylor an unseen glance of jealousy.

"As well you *should* be, my bespectacled friend," Taylor said. "So, what's next?"

"'Plague' and 'city of blackbirds'," Bobbie Leigh said. "Plague sounds bad. Isn't that what killed so many Europeans back in Medieval days?"

"Bubonic Plague," Pilfree said. For the first time since the game began, a genuine countenance of fear took over. "Or ... Black Death. Killed tens of millions in the mid-1300s. Which explains the connection between 'city of *black*birds' and the *Black* Death."

"It does? How so?" Bobbie Leigh asked.

"Raventon, Bobbie Leigh," Taylor replied. Blythington is telling us that the plague, the Black Death, is in Raventon and is set for release on or around the next blood moon, around ... when do you say, Pilfree?"

"August 7."

"That's ...," Bobbie Leigh said.

"*Four* days," Pilfree finished, shining the flashlight to the mound of shovel-removed dirt. "There's something else down here. Bet you can't guess what it is."

Taylor bent and retrieved a red-wax-sealed envelope, shaking it free of soil. Opening it, she read.

"'In the tower of time, somewhere near its top, I have placed three jars. In two of these three jars are thousands of tropical rat fleas, each infected with the pneumonic Plague bacteria. Failure to locate these jars and remove them from the tower of time will activate a device that breaks the jars, releasing the infected fleas. The tower of time is not normally accessible by the public and will require your ingenuity in order to gain access. You have until midnight of the next Blood Moon. Use all means at your disposal. There will be no second chances.

"'Once you have secured the jars, bring them to Unique Antiques and place them at the front door. Await further instructions from that point.'"

"Oh, *no problem!*" Bobbie Leigh said, raising her arms in disgust. "We've *got* this one!"

"Put the dirt back, please, Pilfree," Taylor said, sighing. "Time for some strategy. My house, tomorrow, after breakfast."

19

Variables and Such

"I'm gonna need some help with my algebra homework, Pil-boy!" Bobbie Leigh shouted as Pilfree leaned his bike into the ninety-degree turn to Taylor's driveway.

"What is it about slope-intercept that you don't get?" Pilfree replied as he dismounted his bike and lowered its kickstand.

"Let's see now," Bobbie Leigh said, peeling open the closed fingers of her right fist. "There's the slope part. There's the intercept part. There's the 'mx + b' part and why that side of the equation equals 'y', not to mention the confusion of 'b' representing the 'y' intercept. I'm running out of fingers. Letters, too."

"Because," Pilfree explained, "if you represent the y-intercept part in the equation with the letter 'y', then you'd have the same variable representing two different unknowns on two sides of the equation, and ... then ... well ..."

"Now you know what confusion feels like."

"How about the pay-attention part," Pilfree said.

"Can't. Too busy picking up my brains from the floor."

"*That* shouldn't take you very long."

"Okay, you two," Taylor interceded, "we need to focus on this challenge. Algebra's going to have to take a backseat for now."

"These challenges are sort of like algebra," Pilfree suggested, "wouldn't you say? Variables, unknowns and such."

"How 'bout I intercept your chin with the slope of my fist," Bobbie Leigh said. "*That* I understand."

"So, what exactly is this tower of time, anyway," Taylor asked.

"Sounds clock-ish to me," Pilfree said.

"The clock tower, of course," Bobbie Leigh offered.

"Of course," Pilfree agreed, " but that thing's *never* open. Ever."

"But my Dad ...," Taylor said, eyes widened by the epiphany, "has a *key*."

"Your *dad*? How'd *that* happen?"

"Last spring, he remodeled the interior, repaired the old clock's gears and got the thing working properly again."

"So he *kept* the key?"

"They ... let him, Bobbie Leigh. He has a long-term contract to provide as-needed maintenance on that clock. Letting him have a key saves time, I guess."

"Saves *us* time, too," Pilfree added. "Can you get that key?"

"Don't see why not." Taylor paused in thought. "Okay, we're helping Bobbie Leigh with her algebra, tonight, at your house, BL."

"What?" Bobbie Leigh said, shocked by the abrupt turn. "I thought you said algebra was taking a backseat now."

"And so it is. Your parents are out of town, right?"

"As usual. Out of the country, actually."

"Perfect," Taylor answered. "Let's meet at Bobbie Leigh's house, seven o'clock. We're going to go about solving a few variables of our own."

20

The Key

"Mom, I'm going over to Bobbie Leigh's. Algebra tutoring."

"Don't be too late, Taylor," Susan said. "How's Bobbie Leigh doing with algebra?"

"It's, shall we say ... a real *challenge* for her."

"Well, you're just the one to help. What about supper?"

"Bobbie Leigh's having pizza delivered."

"Home by ten, sweetie."

"Right, Mom. Later!"

Taylor entered the foyer and detoured left into Mike's office. Aware her Dad's desk seemed possessed of evil spirits, its drawer often squealing such spirits' tortured existence each time someone opened it, Taylor pulled the drawer slowly, muffling the groans of its movement with the other hand. Not one for organizational skills, Mike's idea of drawer neatness was a scattering of number two pencils, a few sheets of Christmas seals, a spilled box of paperclips, business cards, and several dollars' worth of coins. Not a key in site.

"Taylor!" Mike shouted as he descended the curving staircase. Taylor pushed shut the drawer, a Pandora's Box of groans and squeals spilling forth.

"Yes, Dad?"

"Oh, there you are," he said, turning the corner. "You're going to Bobbie Leigh's?"

"Helping her with ... with algebra."

"Can you drop this off?" Mike said, reaching for the drawer. "It's for her dad. My bid for work they're having done to remodel their kitchen. Bid's right here, in my desk."

"Sure, Dad. I'll make sure she gets it."

"She?"

"Bobbie Leigh's parents are out of town."

"Oh, that's right. France," he remembered, shoving the Request for Bid document back into his desk drawer. "I'll drop it off for them next week. Thanks, Taylor."

"Sure thing, Dad. By the way, isn't it ... isn't it a bit warm for hoodies?"

"You know mom and her a/c settings," he replied.

"You bet I do. Okay, see ya."

Taylor watched Mike return upstairs, his hooded shadow advancing, eventually fading from view around the stairs' turns. Again, she pulled carefully the drawer.

"Where *is* it?" she whispered, moving aside the clutter of items. "Ah, under the seals. Let's go, you."

Taylor tucked the key into her jeans pocket and slipped her backpack over her right shoulder. Closing the front door, she climbed aboard her bike and checked the time.

4:35.

Twenty-five minutes to get the key copied and put back into her dad's desk.

21

Real-time Problem-solving

"Now that we're here, any bright ideas, strategy-wise?" Bobbie Leigh asked.

Taylor reached into her jeans pocket and pulled out a shiny brass key. "Strategy would be a lot easier if you had ordered some pizza."

"Won't your dad know it's missing?" Pilfree asked, taking the key from Taylor's fingers.

"Not a chance," Taylor answered. "Had a copy made."

"Aren't you the clever one!"

"And speaking of strategy, Bobbie Leigh, here's some."

"Really? Do tell!"

"Okay," Taylor whispered, curling her arms around the shoulders of her friends. "We go to the tower, right?"

"To the tower, yes. Then what?"

"We take *this* key," Taylor said, grabbing it from Pilfree's fingers and holding it up, "and we *insert* it into the tower's door lock."

"Sounds good so far, Taylor," Pilfree whispered, awaiting the revelation of a master plan.

"We *turn* the key, unlocking the door," she whispered, "and enter *through* the unlocked tower door, closing it behind us."

Pilfree and Bobbie Leigh stared at Taylor.

"Why are we whispering?" Pilfree asked.

"*And* ...," Bobbie Leigh said. "Then what?"

"How should *I* know!" Taylor said. "We find the three jars, is what! We take them to Unique Antiques. We await further instructions, is what! We do this before midnight of August 7. In other words, *your* strategy's as good as *mine*."

"So, you're saying you're ... clueless?"

"Bingo!"

"Oh ... well, I guess that's as good a strategy as one can have, given what we know," Pilfree said.

"Of *course* it is," Taylor said. "This part isn't complicated. What we do *not* know is where those three jars are located. *That's* when we'll need strategy, because who knows *how* Blythington has rigged the jars to break should we fail to find and remove them on time."

"Real-time problem-solving."

"Exactly, Pilfree. That's what these challenges have been all about. Thinking on our feet. Applying our knowledge and our teamwork as we go. Persevering; not surrendering. And now we are under the severest of time constraints. That is precisely why we have to stop the insults, the arguing, the personal jabs. One slip-up, especially at this point of the game, could cost lives, namely our *own*. And I'm in no frame of mind to second-guess Blythington's seriousness, what he *will* or will *not* do. Twisted as this game and Blythington may be, we are in it for keeps."

"Well, *not me*. Not anymore!"

Pilfree and Taylor turned to Bobbie Leigh and glanced at each other, eyebrows raised.

"This is *stupid!*" Bobbie Leigh announced.

"Stupid?"

"Taylor, *look* at us," Bobbie Leigh said, a sob in her voice. "We've become puppets, Blythington's puppets, dancing on strings of his pulling. And for *what?* To preserve our lives? *Really?* And how do we know the puppet master *is* Blythington WonVillingham? As far as I'm concerned, he's long dead. Someone has assumed his identity and is using us for some sick game of intimidation. We've fallen for it, hook, line, and stinker!"

"Sinker," Pilfree corrected.

"*Whatever!* I refuse to believe anymore that our lives are at risk if we fail to follow the letter of these challenges."

"But, Bobbie Leigh–"

"No more!"

The three stood silent for a moment.

"I'm going home," Bobbie Leigh said.

"Uh, Bobbie Leigh ..." Pilfree said.

"What!"

"You're *already* home," Taylor said.

Bobbie Leigh noticed the familiar surroundings of home. "Yes, well ... then I'm taking a walk, to clear my mind."

"That ought to be the longest walk in history," Pilfree whispered, unheard.

"Pilfree had a *tree* fall on him," Taylor said, "back at the cemetery, just after we'd told him about this game. What if Pilfree had not won the Rubik's Cube contest; you two might never have found me at Sagitaw Falls. Now there might be plague-infested fleas! Is that a chance you're willing to take?"

Bobbie Leigh bowed her head. She said nothing.

"So, Bobbie Leigh," Taylor suggested as she twirled the key in her fingers, "why don't we take a stroll over to the clock tower? Not a better place to clear one's mind."

22

The Challenge of Jars

"When was this thing built?" Pilfree asked, his head in full upward slant toward the clock tower's lighted top. "Look's prehistoric!"

"Practically is," Bobbie Leigh agreed. "Got any more of those poptarts, Pil-boy?"

"Nope. All eaten. But glad you've taken a shine to them."

"So, what's eating *you*, Bobbie Leigh?" Taylor asked.

"Like I said, I'm tired of playing this so-called game. What's it good for, anyway? I want out."

"But Bobbie Leigh, we've come so far. We've conquered every challenge. We've worked together by using each other's strengths. We've become a true team."

"Right, and *one* slip-up, and we're *dead?*"

"Which is precisely why we have to see this thing through, Bobbie Leigh," Pilfree said, as if it needed saying. "That, and the reward waiting for us after all challenges have been met."

"Which brings me to that," Bobbie Leigh replied. "*What* reward? A pat on the back? A twenty-dollar gift card to Unique Antiques? A year's supply of *poptarts?*"

Taylor pulled her backpack off her shoulder and unzipped the main pocket. "Here's a little reminder, something BJW mentioned in the original document found inside the radio, and I quote, '*But, should you proceed, following to the letter each detail of each instruction, when completed your rewards will eclipse any of your expectations and in ways that will utterly and positively alter your lives and the lives of many others.*'"

"Pretty powerful incentive to carry on, I'd say," Pilfree said.

"But *what* rewards? I don't have *any* expectations, never did. Does that then mean our rewards are *nothing*?"

"I'm game for any rewards that will, as he states, 'alter your lives'."

"Didn't he also mention something about a red satin ribbon, that we'd *need* it?" Bobbie Leigh asked.

"He did," Taylor replied.

"So, do you still *have* said red satin ribbon?"

"Right here," Taylor answered. "Wonder what he has in mind for it."

He'll tell us when the time's ripe, I'm sure," Pilfree said.

"So," Taylor said with a sigh and holding up the key, light from the full moon shimmering off it, "shall we?"

"We shall," Pilfree replied, rubbing his hands together.

"Bobbie Leigh?"

"Yeah, okay ... let's do this."

Taylor inserted the key and turned it leftward. Pressing her shoulder against the thick oak wood, she gave the door a controlled push, expecting it to emit groans similar to her dad's desk, only on a magnitude that might wake the dead. As it opened, air rushed into their faces, air filled with the smells of one hundred and forty-two years of aged age; of human comings and goings; of the sustained movements of oiled, geared machinery; and of its ghostly occupants.

The clock tower's dimensions were some twenty-five feet in width at its base by a hundred and thirty feet tall. A spiral staircase filled the tower's center, leading up to the old clock and a circular observation deck.

Flashlight shining, Taylor led the way up. Six shoes shuffled their scraping sounds along the metal steps.

"So, are we looking for the jars of bubonic-plagued fleas yet?" Pilfree asked. "Want to venture a guess where they might be?"

"Could be anywhere, I suppose," Taylor replied. "Just be careful where you place your hands."

"Don't have to tell me that twice," Bobbie Leigh said as she pocketed her hands.

"AHH!" Pilfree shouted.

"What?"

"Spiders, Taylor! *There.* Big ones."

"Spiders!" Bobbie Leigh said. "Where? I *hate* spiders!

"They're *all over* these walls! *Little* ones, too."

"Ain't no such thing as a *little* spider."

"They're harmless, guys," Taylor said, unconvincingly.

"Yeah?" Bobbie Leigh said. "And how about that *humongous* spider in that web directly in front of you?"

Taylor shone her light onto the web, the center of which lurked a massive brown-and-black spider, its legs in full extension.

"Oh my God!"

"*Now* what?" Pilfree said.

"Got anything in your backpack for *that*, Taylor?" Bobbie Leigh asked.

Taylor gave the web a quick poke with the flashlight. She gave it another, even quicker poke.

"Did you *see* that?" Taylor said.

"See *what?*" Bobbie Leigh replied.

"Exactly!" Taylor answered. "It didn't move."

"And your point?"

Taylor reached with her hand, placing it firmly onto the web.

"Taylor!" Pilfree shouted.

Bobbie Leigh gasped.

Taylor smiled. "It's *fake!* The spider's not real."

"You mean ..."

"Exactly. Blythington's rigged the place, trying to scare us away."

"And the spiders on the walls ...?" Pilfree asked.

"Fake, too. See?" Taylor said, picking the sticky spiders off the wall. One spider on her fingers crawled up Taylor's palm to her wrist. Calmly, she shook it off. "Okay, *most* are fake."

The three continued their climb, vigilant of eight-legged critters, real or fake. As they stepped onto the interior platform that extended to the observation deck outside, the clock's massive mechanics loomed before them, gears clicking uninterrupted, ticking off the seconds of time. Taped to the wall, they found an envelope sealed with red wax. On its outside were scrawled the words: **Supplement to Challenge #7.**

"*Supplement?*" Bobbie Leigh said, spotting the envelope. "Like the main challenges aren't enough?"

Taylor removed the envelope from the wall, broke the wax seal, and opened it. Clearing her throat, she opened her mouth to read: "'I hope you have Fragment 83'".

Taylor stopped.

"Do you?" she asked.

"Right here," Pilfree answered, patting his backpack.

Taylor continued: "'In the workings of this old clock is a part that strongly resembles this Fragment 83. Behind that clock part you will find three glass jars and one pendulum. First, you must remove this part. Don't worry; this part is no longer a functional part of the clock's workings, so its removal does no harm to the clock. The only tool you will need for its removal is a set of hands. After removing this part, replace it with Fragment 83. You must then remove each jar from left to right without touching the passing pendulum. The pendulum, by the way, has been manipulated so that from the moment you entered the tower, each pass of the pendulum has drawn it nearer to the row of jars. Eventually, its path will take it directly into the space occupied by the row of jars. Any jars, or jar, not removed will be pushed off the platform to its shattering demise below, its contents released upon Raventon.'

"'Furthermore, one touch of the pendulum by you, ever so slightly, will result in the left-most jar being pushed off its pedestal and down to the floor far below. The jar will shatter, its contents released upon Raventon.'

"'Two of the three jars contain hundreds of thousands of plague-diseased fleas. One jar contains air only. There is no way for you to know which jar contains air only, so you must exercise total care in each jar's removal. If a jar does happen to fall, you might know sooner rather than later whether it contained air ... or plague.

"'Remember, you are looking for a clock part that strongly resembles Fragment 83. Oh, and one last thing: Upon removal of the clock part resembling Fragment 83, you will see before you a web occupied by a spider, this one very big and very real and very poisonous. Place Fragment 83 here. Thought you'd want to know. I am certain you can ... handle it.'"

Silence overwhelmed the tower space, interrupted only by the pounding of three hearts.

"Let's see the fragment, Pilfree," Taylor said.

Pilfree removed the plastic bag from his backpack and from the plastic bag, Fragment 83.

"Wow. So *this* is from the Antikythera Mechanism?" Taylor asked.

"So says Blythington," Pilfree replied.

"Looks rather gear-ish, like the rest of the Antikythera mechanism."

"And like the *rest* of this old clock!" Bobbie Leigh observed. "And I ain't dealing with no *real* spider!"

"How will we know which part?" Pilfree asked, looking at the many clock gears.

"Easy," Taylor replied.

"*Easy?* You mean all we have to do is find the poisonous spider!" Bobbie Leigh said.

"All we have to do is find the *pendulum*, which is right over *there*," Taylor said, pointing with her flashlight to the swift to-and-fro movement of the long pendulum. "The part we're looking for ought to be right in front of it. In fact, I think I see it now."

"Great grimy gopher guts!" Pilfree said, spotting the same object.

"So, who's going to remove the part, assuming *that's* the part?" Bobbie Leigh said. "Remember, I do *not* do spiders!"

"Let's see just what's involved with removing the part," Taylor answered.

"Blythington said all we'd need is a set of hands," Pilfree said. "Any set, I presume."

The three approached the pendulum, wary with every step the presence of any renegade spider. Taylor handed the flashlight to Pilfree and gripped the part.

"Looks *exactly* like Fragment 83," Pilfree observed. "In fact, except for size, I can't tell the difference. Same inscriptions. Both look like gears with a lot of teeth, only ours is greener, rustier."

"Just like your brain," Bobbie Leigh said. "Then this *must* be the part, Pil-boy."

"Here goes nothing," Taylor said as she pulled on the part. The part lifted almost effortlessly from the hold of a slot. "That was easy. See any spider?"

"Not even a web," Pilfree replied.

"But Blythington said there was a spider," Bobbie Leigh said, eyes peering right to left and back again. "It may be hiding."

"And Blythington may be lying," Taylor said.

"Spiders react to any disturbance of their web, usually by attacking the disturber, killing it, and encasing it in its web for future consumption," Pilfree said.

"They should rename Google in honor of you, call it 'Pil-boy'," Bobbie Leigh said, amused by her attempt to lighten her anxiety.

"Point is, Bobbie Leigh," Pilfree explained, "there was *no* reaction because there is *no* web because there is *no* spider! Blythington's playing with our fears, just like he warned us he would." Pilfree placed Fragment 83 in the slot vacated by the part.

"Not all big spiders *build* webs," Bobbie Leigh said.

"There're the jars," Taylor said, with a forward nod of her head, drawing attention away from spiders.

The three jars rested, twelve inches space between each, on a two-feet-by-two-feet iron platform atop a metal post, one arm's-length's reach away from the railing, depending on whose arm did the reaching. The pendulum, probably five feet in length, swished by the jars at a rate of one pass per second. The monotonous clicking of gears filled their ears. Time marched onward, despite their desires that it stand still, for just a while.

The glass of each jar had been smeared with the smudge of smoke, obscuring any view of the contents within. Two of the three jars contained deadly plague-carrying fleas, but which two?

"If the poisonous spider was a ruse, maybe the fleas are as well?" Pilfree offered, unconvinced of his own thought.

"And you're willing to take that chance?" Taylor replied.

"You've got the longest arm, Pilfree," Bobbie Leigh said.

"Think you can reach the jars," Taylor asked.

Pilfree sighed. "Timing is everything. Let me give this a test or two."

Pilfree lay on his stomach and slithered to the deck's edge opposite the jars and platform. Ever mindful of the passing pendulum, its swing fanning his face, Pilfree cocked his arm. He thrust his arm forward as the pendulum passed, pulling it back immediately.

"That wasn't too bad, Pilfree," Taylor said, "but grabbing a jar, holding onto it no less and pulling it back, is going to ... well ... think you can manage it?"

"Have you forgotten how fast I can solve a Rubic's Cube?" he answered with a question.

"But that's using *fingers*, Pilfree," Bobbie Leigh said.

"And just what are fingers attached to, my dear?"

"Hands, of course," Bobbie Leigh answered.

"And hands to arms. I *got* this, y'all!"

"Well and good, my friend, but don't mind me while I hold my breath," Bobbie Leigh said.

"Do good, Pilfree," Taylor said, patting his back.

Pilfree spat into his hands and rubbed them together. Puzzled, Bobbie Leigh and Taylor stared at Pilfree.

"I got sticky spit," he said. "Like a dog's."

"That explains a lot," Bobbie Leigh whispered.

"On three, Pilfree," Taylor said.

"On three," he confirmed.

"One ... two ..."

"Wait!"

"*What*, Pil-boy!" Bobbie Leigh said.

"Got an itch, left shoulder blade."

Taylor bent to her knees and scratched the area.

"A little lower ... little lower ... a bit to the right ... yes, *there*. Thanks!"

"Take two," Bobbie Leigh said, rolling her eyes. "Would you like a poptart first?"

"Wouldn't hurt."

"We better get this done," Taylor observed. "Pendulum's getting closer to the jars. On three."

"On three," Pilfree said, taking one last deep breath.

"One ... two ... *three!*"

With that, Pilfree extended his left arm forward, just as the pendulum passed, his fingers tightening around the first jar. He pulled back his arm. The pendulum's passing pushed a strand of hair across his forehead.

Bobbie Leigh released her carbon dioxide-filled lungs. "Well *done,* doofus!"

"Indeed, well done, Pilfree," Taylor added.

"Don't open it!" Bobbie Leigh shouted.

"I was just checking to see–"

"You were checking to *see?*"

"Oh, yeah ... *that*."

"Pilfree, how can *stupidity* and *brilliance* coexist so peacefully?" Bobbie Leigh said.

"Me being me," Pilfree replied.

"Be somebody *else* for a change!"

"*Chill*, you two," Taylor intervened. "We've *got* to work together, support each other. Ready for number two, Pilfree?"

"As I'll ever be," he replied.

"Good. On three."

"On three." Pilfree knelt and lay on his stomach.

"Ready?" Taylor said, her eyes honing the timing of the pendulum's passes. "One ... two ... *three!*"

Pilfree thrust his arm forward, this time catching his thumb on the iron railing.

"AHHH!"

The pendulum edged nearer to the two remaining jars.

"Pilfree!" Bobbie Leigh said. "Are you okay?"

"As if you cared," Pilfree replied, squeezing his thumb.

"Are you hurt, Pilfree?" Taylor asked.

"Feels like it."

"Let me see it."

"Feels sprained, maybe broken," he said.

"Swelling up, too," Taylor added. "I'm betting it's broken."

"Oh, *great*," Bobbie Leigh said.

"See if either of you can reach the jars," Pilfree suggested.

Taylor stretched out on her stomach and reached forward.

"Too ... too short, Pilfree," she said.

Bobbie Leigh tried. She stretched her fingers out, coming up short by at least two inches.

"What now?" Bobbie Leigh asked.

"It's got to be *you*, Pilfree, broken thumb or no," Taylor said.

Pilfree sighed. He lay on his stomach.

"I'll use my right arm this time."

"On three?" Bobbie Leigh said, wanting to do the counting this time.

"On three."

"One ... two ... *three!*"

Pilfree reached in but could not grab hold of jar number two. Thinking quickly, he withdrew his arm at the precise instant the pendulum swished by, barely avoiding touching it.

"Wow, *that* was close!" Bobbie Leigh said.

"Thumb hurts like the *Dickens*."

"Gotta ignore it," Taylor said. "Let's try again."

"Can we do this on four?" Pilfree asked.

"On four, then," Taylor acknowledged. "Count it, Bobbie Leigh."

"One ... two ... three ... *four!*"

As if possessed, Pilfree reached in and grabbed the second jar, pulling it back to the safety of the observation deck. Cringing in pain, he set it down on its side.

"*Grab it!*" Taylor shouted, as the jar rolled toward the deck's edge.

Bobbie Leigh rushed to the jar and lunged her left foot into the jar's path, stopping its roll. All three sighed. Taylor picked up the jar and placed it out of the way, next to the first jar.

"Two down," Bobbie Leigh said.

"One to go," Pilfree added.

The pendulum's swing was now a half-inch away from striking the third jar.

"You got to get this one, Pilfree," Taylor said. "First attempt."

Pilfree rested his left thumb in the palm of his right hand. The thumb, pulsating in pain, had swollen to the size of a lemon.

"*Hurry*, Pilfree!" shouted Bobbie Leigh. "You get this jar, and I *swear* I will take back *all* the doofuses I've ever called you. Plus the pop fart!"

"But not the Pil-boy?" Pilfree said with a smile.

"Not on your life, my dear," Bobbie Leigh replied softly, returning the smile.

"Consider it done," Pilfree said, spitting into his right hand, rubbing it on his shirt, and stretching prone. "On four ... my dear."

"One ... two ... three ... *AHHH!*"

Just as Bobbie Leigh finished her count, the pendulum finished the unthinkable. It grazed the third jar. On its return swing, the pendulum tapped the jar a bit harder, sending it into an unbalanced topple. Eyes widened in the shock of the moment. The three watched, as if frozen in a slow-motion replay, the jar turning end over end, downward silently into the darkness of the clock tower's innards.

The jar shattered, breaking the silence of their disbelief.

Stilled, they stood for a moment, waiting, seconds like hours, each wondering if the shattered jar indeed contained plague-ridden fleas.

"Do you think–"

"We have a one-in-three chance."

"Or a two-in-three chance, depending on how one views this."

"How do *you* view this, Pilfree," Taylor asked.

"As probably the most frightened I've ever been in my entire life."

"Same here," she replied.

"We're just sitting ducks up here in this tower," Bobbie Leigh said. "If we go down, we risk walking right into a cloud of fleas. If we stay, those same fleas will come to us."

"Pilfree, look at those two jars," Taylor suggested. "Can you see inside them at all?"

Pilfree shone the flashlight on each of the two jars.

"Too smudged," he said.

"Well, we can't stay here," Taylor said as she picked up the jars and placed them inside her backpack. "We have to take these jars to Unique Antiques, per the challenge's instructions. Meanwhile, pray both of them are the jars containing the fleas."

Taylor, Bobbie Leigh, and Pilfree descended the spiral stairs, paying no regard to spiders or their webs. Bobbie Leigh slapped her face.

"What is it, BL?" Taylor asked

"Felt something tickling my cheek; thought it might be a flea."

"Yeah, I'm feeling that same sort of thing. Must be our minds playing tricks on us," Pilfree said, scratching his noggin.

"Hope that's *all* it is," Taylor said.

"I'm sure that's ... all it is."

"There it is," Bobbie Leigh said as she stopped at the bottom of the stairs.

"The glass jar, what's left of it," Pilfree said.

"I'll take these jars home with me," Taylor said. "Meet me at Unique Antiques at 9:00."

"Hey." Bobbie Leigh said, "what's that taped to the door?"

"Must be Blythington's 'further instructions'."

"No," Taylor said, "his 'further instructions' are supposed to be waiting for us at Unique Antiques, which is why we have to get there before they open."

"Why's that?" Bobbie Leigh asked.

"So no one else takes the instructions, including the shop's owner," Pilfree explained. "Remember, Blythington mentioned something in the original game-document's instructions about curiosity killing the cat. We've got to keep the 'curious' away."

"Pilfree's right," Taylor said, "which is why we probably should go there now, to see if those 'further instructions' are posted, like this envelope is."

"So open *this* envelope," Bobbie Leigh said.

Pilfree pulled the envelope from its tape and peeled away the red wax seal. He smiled.

"What's it say?"

"'Time to … flea the scene.' With a winking smiley face."

"Such a wonderful sense of humor he has," Bobbie Leigh said.

Taylor locked the oak door behind them, and the three began their scratch-filled sprint to Unique Antiques.

23

Unique Antiques

(or just another flea market?)

"It just occurred to me," Bobbie Leigh said.

"What occurred to you?"

"Let me see that last message, the one taped to the clock tower door."

Taylor took the folded paper from her pocket. "Here you go."

Bobbie Leigh unfolded the paper. "Weird."

"You mean, something other than you?" Pilfree said, smiling.

Bobbie Leigh ignored the remark. "Upper left corner," she said.

Taylor and Pilfree looked to where Bobbie Leigh's finger pointed. In small Old English font were the words, **Unique Antiques, 262 Main Street, Raventon, GA 30001**

"It's Unique Antique's letterhead," Taylor said.

"What's that smudge below the letterhead," Bobbie Leigh asked.

"Looks ... looks like maybe a smushed gnat," Pilfree said.

"Or a smushed *flea*," Taylor countered.

"So, why's this message on Unique Antiques letterhead," Bobbie Leigh asked.

"Good question," answered Taylor. "Maybe there are more challenges?"

"I guess we'll know soon enough."

"There's the shop," Pilfree said.

"Look for another envelope, probably taped to a window or the door."

A slight glow appeared on the eastern horizon, giving notice of the arrival of a new day.

"Oh, man, my parents have got to be so worried," Taylor said, having lost all notice of time. "I told them I was helping you with algebra, Bobbie Leigh. And that I'd be home by ten."

"So, it took longer than you thought," Bobbie Leigh said, adjusting her hair.

"Mom never expected me to spend the night, Bobbie Leigh. She *would* have expected a heads-up phone call."

"So, call her now, tell her that slope-intercept is a lot harder for me than you thought it'd be."

"But, that would be—"

"*Not* lying! Slope-intercept truly is one of life's mysteries, Taylor, almost as weird as this *walking mystery* known as the Doofus. Tell her we ... took a stroll to ... to *clear my mind!* After all, that *was* your idea."

"Mom's probably tried calling your parents."

"Neither of whom are home. Here, give me that phone."

Bobbie Leigh took Taylor's cell phone and pecked in Taylor's parents' number. Pilfree continued his search for 'further instructions'.

"Mrs. Smart? Bobbie Leigh Harwell here ... hold on, Mrs. S, hold on ... yes, she's *fine*, she's right here with me, and ... *don't worry* ... yes, you can speak to her, but I wanted you to hear it from me ... yes, and algebra for me is like the *hardest subject* on the planet, all those letters and junk ... yes, ma'am, here's Taylor."

Bobbie Leigh handed Taylor the phone. Taylor felt a nagging discomfort shroud her conscience as the conversation evolved, that of affirming Bobbie Leigh's account, knowing that such was at best an extreme stretching of the truth and at worst was an outright lie. She apologized to her mom, finding remorse a plentiful commodity, but she managed to make Bobbie Leigh's story believable. Taylor mitigated her discomfort by convincing herself she would settle up with her mom later.

"Found it!" Pilfree blurted.

"Really? Where was it?"

"Under the doormat, of all places," he said, handing the envelope to Taylor.

"Glad you thought to look there, Pilfree," Bobbie Leigh said.

"I guess Blythington, too, didn't want to risk his further instructions falling into the hands of the curious," Taylor said.

"So, what are the further instructions?" Pilfree asked.

"The sixty-four thousand dollar question, my friend."

"The ... *what?*" Bobbie Leigh said, her brows furrowed.

"Never mind," Pilfree answered. "What does he want us to do now, Taylor?"

Taylor opened the envelope, then stopped and looked away, eyes closed.

"What's wrong, Taylor?" Bobbie Leigh asked.

"Don't know, Bobbie Leigh. I suddenly feel ... very weak ... and nauseous."

"Probably because you haven't eaten since lunch yesterday."

"Probably." Taylor cleared her throat and tried to return her focus to the envelope of further instructions. She couldn't shake the thought that she'd not felt this poorly since her chemo treatments for leukemia some six years ago. Again clearing her throat, she read.

"Says, 'After the shop opens, give the jars to the shop owner. If you have returned unbroken three jars, then the game is completed, and the official Declarer of Outcomes will crown you as winners. If, however, you have returned two jars, you must wait until the contents of the two jars can be confirmed. If one of the two jars contains air only, then the Declarer of Outcomes must assume the third jar was broken, releasing the plagued fleas upon Raventon and the entire region. If the two jars both contain fleas, the Declarer of Outcomes will crown you as winners of the game. I needn't explain to you the outcome if you have returned only one jar. If the Declarer of Outcomes deems you winners of the game, you must await your reward within the shop.'

"Okay. There you ... have it. Um, I have ... I have to sit down, y'all."

"Here, Taylor," Pilfree said, taking Taylor's arm and leading her to a sidewalk bench, "sit here."

"I don't ... I don't know what's happening here," Taylor whispered.

"Drink this." Bobbie Leigh put a bottle of water to Taylor's lips and tilted it so a trickle of water entered her mouth. Taylor took two swallows of the water after which she slumped to her left, unconscious, onto the bench.

"Taylor!" Bobbie Leigh cried.

Bobbie Leigh took Taylor's phone and pressed '911'.

"Call her mom, Pilfree," she shouted.

24

The Declarer of Outcomes

As the ambulance pulled away, with Taylor Smart and her parents aboard, the clock tower chimed its eight-o'clock bells, each bong a stinging reminder of the night before and the possibilities yet to come.

Bobbie Leigh and Pilfree stayed behind. Nothing to do but wait, wait for the shop to open; wait for the outcome of the challenge game; wait for knowledge of Taylor's condition. Maybe they had not followed the rules of the game to the letter. Maybe they had not worked as the team Blythington WonVillingham had expected. Maybe Taylor's condition was a hint of the game's deadly consequences, even though the so-called Declarer of Outcomes had not yet made the decision official.

Unique Antiques opened in an hour. Not enough time to go home, to get some rest, maybe some breakfast, but too much time to sit waiting on the edge of a sidewalk bench, on the brink of a future uncertain.

"Look there," Pilfree said.

A man wearing a black hoodie and baggy black jeans, his head tilted downward, the hood framing his face such that his features were concealed, approached the shop. He shuffled his shoes along the concrete, his choppy strides barely lifting them as he walked. He stopped in front of Pilfree and Bobbie Leigh, head down, his face shadowed by the oversized hood topping his head.

"The jars, please," he said with what sounded like an electronically doctored voice, as if he were speaking through a device that did such. No such device was visibly evident, yet the man spoke as might a robot.

"The jars, please," he repeated, hands extended.

Bobbie Leigh stared, eyes wide as saucers and just as unblinking. Pilfree said nothing. He took the jars from the bench he had set them on and handed them to the man.

The hooded man, hands clothed in black leather, took the jars, slipped them inside his oversized hoodie, and walked toward the shop's door. Bobbie Leigh and Pilfree watched but could not see what he was doing. Then, the door opened, and the man disappeared within, shutting the door behind him.

"*Who* was *that?*" Bobbie Leigh asked.

"Your guess is as good as mine. I have to assume he has something to do with the game."

"Well, *duh!*" Bobbie Leigh said, "but is *that* the Declarer of Outcomes?"

"Could be," Pilfree replied, "or it just may be the messenger."

"The messenger?"

"Taking the jars to the Declarer of Outcomes."

"So we wait?"

"We wait," Pilfree said, sitting on the bench. "Can't help but think about Taylor. What do you suppose—"

"I don't want to suppose anything. Think a plague flea bit her?"

"Doubtful, even if that broken jar contained them."

"Why not?"

"Too soon, Bobbie Leigh. The bacteria need several days, maybe six days, to incubate."

"Then what's *wrong* with her?"

"Didn't want to mention it, but I hope it's not a recurrence of her leukemia."

"Oh my *God*, I hadn't thought of that."

"Have a seat, Bobbie Leigh. Nothing we can do but wait."

"Do you have your cell phone?"

"I do," Pilfree said, pulling it from his pocket. "One bar."

"Call Taylor's mom. Maybe she can tell us something."

"Bobbie Leigh, it's too soon. She's probably not at the hospital yet."

"Bet her mom knows. Call her."

"I don't know ..."

"Pilfree, your phone has *one* sinkin' bar. If you don't call *now*–"

"Stinkin'."

"What?"

"*Stinkin'* bar. You said sinkin'."

"It *is* sinkin', getting *lower* by the minute. Call *now*. We may not have another chance."

Reluctantly, Pilfree agreed. As he pecked the numbers, a hooded head emerged from the slightly opened front door of Unique Antiques.

"Pilfree? Bobbie Leigh?" the robotic voice said.

"That's us," Bobbie Leigh answered.

"Step inside, please. Remove your shoes and proceed to the center of the shop. There you will find cushions on which to sit. Sit. Wait. The Declarer of Outcomes has reached the decision."

Bobbie Leigh looked at Pilfree who maintained his face-forward stare.

"How's your thumb feeling, Pil-boy?"

"Bobbie Leigh," Pilfree said, chin lifted, "there comes a time in a person's life when thumbs no longer matter."

"So who are you paraphrasing now?"

"General Winfield Scott Hancock, commander of the Union Second Corps at Gettysburg."

"O ... kay. I take it your thumb's killing you."

"And *how*. C'mon, let's go inside."

Both entered the shop and slowly made their way to a circle of cushions on the floor in the middle of the shop. The hooded man closed and locked the front door.

In the circle's center, atop an iron tripod pedestal, burned the wick of a thick candle, its sides adorned with both the running and frozen melt of wax. At a point along the arc of the circle of cushions was a throne-like chair with lion-clawed feet, its entirety carved of thick wood worn smooth by centuries of use, its seat, armrests and back bearing pillows of purple satin.

"Sit," the hooded man said.

After a few long minutes, a man robed as one might expect of a monk entered from behind a red drape hanging over an opening to a rear room, darkness obscuring the room's contents and purpose. He took his place in the throne-like chair and removed his hood.

"You do not know me, but I know you," the wrinkled man said slowly, deeply. "You will speak only when asked to speak. You will listen always."

The man reached into his robe's pocket and pulled out a legal-sized envelope, red-wax-sealed. Breaking the seal, he removed a multi-paged vellum document.

"This," he said, "is the Last Will and Testament of one Blythington Jehosiphats WonVillingham. Mr. WonVillingham died April 21, 1975. It has taken forty years for the terms of his will to come to fruition. Congratulations, my young friends. Fate has chosen you. As Declarer of Outcomes, I hereby pronounce you ... winners of Mr. WonVillingham's ... game."

Pilfree turned to Bobbi Leigh, not sure if he should laugh or cry or maybe just shout to the four winds. He remained silent, smiling, having not been prompted to speak.

"That's what *I'm* talking about!" shouted Bobbie Leigh, lifting her hands to receive a high-five from Pilfree.

"Bobbie Leigh, *shhhh!*" whispered Pilfree.

"The jar shattered at the clock tower contained air only. As for your friend, your teammate without whom none of you would be here now, she is very sick. Very sick, indeed. The reward for your successful efforts is contained within this Last Will and Testament of one Blythington Jehosiphats WonVillingham.

"Before I reveal to you the terms of the Will and the specifics of your reward, including its distribution, have you questions?"

"*Have* we!" Bobbie Leigh shouted, her balloon of frustration exploding.

"*Bobbie Leigh!*"

"Well, Pilfree, he *asked*. And now *I'm* gonna ask!"

"Proceed, young friend," the man said.

"*Who* is Blythington WonVillingham?"

"All you need to know is that Mr. WonVillingham earned a considerable fortune in shipping, rail and maritime. He was met with challenge after challenge in his lifetime, never faltering in the face of such. Mr. WonVillingham had two children, boys, who expected to inherit their father's fortune, as Mr. WonVillingham had inherited his seed fortune from his father. They never tried earning fortunes of their own; they resisted any challenge and opportunity given them. Because of his sons' passivity, Mr. WonVillingham denied them their birthright, a birthright he would have lovingly relinquished had his sons shown a genuine measure of appreciation of the requisite hard work.

"Mr. WonVillingham and his sons remained estranged for the remainder of the time they shared on this planet. He carried his profound disappointment with him to his grave. His sons have been deceased for thirty-eight years, having died in the 1977 crash of airliners on the runway at Tenerife, in the Canary Islands.

"Mr. WonVillingham preserved his fortune in his Will, hidden within his favorite radio, the Stromberg-Carlson floor model belonging to Mr. WonVillingham's sister and purchased here by Taylor's mom. His intent was that his fortune might be earned, if his Will were ever discovered, only by the one—or, in your case, ones—willing to take seriously and accept the terms of his unique game of challenges. You did, and here you are. Next question."

"If we had failed to perform the challenges as instructed," Pilfree said, carefully gathering his thought, "would we *really* have lost our lives? Murder seems rather extreme, don't you think?"

"The positive and negative incentives of Mr. Blythington's game served their intended purpose, their means to a specific end. The answer you seek no longer matters, for you have accomplished the desired end. One more question."

Bobbie Leigh took this one. "How in the name of saltpeter did *whoever* know our *every* move and each challenge's outcome, before even *we* knew them?"

"That is a question for the ages, young friend. Someday, perhaps you will know."

"But ..."

"No more questions concerning Mr. WonVillingham or the game. Item 1 ..."

Pilfree lifted his hand no higher than his ear in a silent request to speak.

"What is your question?"

"I ... *we* ... are very worried about Taylor. Can you tell us more about her condition?"

The man sighed. "Taylor Smart has experienced a very severe relapse with her leukemia, specifically juvenile myelomonocytic leukemia. Without immediate chemotherapy, followed by bone marrow transplants ... she will not survive."

Bobbie Leigh gasped, tears forming.

"She mentioned feeling weak during this game," Pilfree recalled, "as if something was pulling her energy from her."

"Will ... will she live?" Bobbie Leigh asked.

"She will have to endure several weeks of chemotherapy, which will likely destroy her immune system, increasing her risk of infections. But the chemo will also destroy the cancerous cells as well, and she'll receive the necessary treatments to fend off infections. Then, she will need a bone marrow transplant, stem cells harvested from her and her dad six years ago, for such a recurrence as this. The outcome is fraught with uncertainty, but it's the best hope she has."

"When can we see her?" Bobbie Leigh asked.

"Give her a week, at least, before visiting, but do nothing without her parents' permission. Now, let me give you some good news."

"Unless it's news of Taylor's full recovery, it's not news worth hearing," Bobbie Leigh said.

"It's news that could *mean* full recovery."

"Then, let's hear it," Pilfree said.

"Item 1: Being of sound mind–"

"*Sound mind?*" Bobbie Leigh said. "*Weird* mind, at best!"

"Bobbie Leigh, let him *finish*," Pilfree whispered.

"Item 1: Being of sound mind, I bequeath to the winner, or winners, of my challenge game the sum, to be divided evenly in the event of multiple winners, of three hundred fifty million dollars.

"Item 2 ..."

"Wait," Bobbie Leigh said, jaw extended towards the cushion on which she sat. "*What?*"

"I gotta admit, sir," Pilfree said, "I didn't quite get that myself. Did you say ... three hundred fifty million ... *dollars?*"

"That I did. Now, if I may continue."

"Divided three ways," Bobbie Leigh whispered, "that's like ... ninety million *each!*"

"More like one hundred sixteen million, six hundred sixty-seven thousand ... each," Pilfree corrected. "I see you must have slept through *that* lesson as well."

"Ahem!" the man said. "*May* I?"

"Certainly, sir," Pilfree said. "Our apologies. It's just that it's not everyday that–"

"No, it isn't, but you'll want to hear the rest. Item 2: The remainder of my estate, plus any interest and appreciation earned on said estate from the point of my death until this point, the book value of which exceeds six hundred fifty million dollars, is to be donated to funding the charity or charities of the winner(s)' choice but is restricted only to charities that advance the human condition in ways positive, but must not support any political agenda. You have thirty minutes to determine which charity or charities will be the beneficiary(ies) of my estate, but *both* of you must agree. After said amount of time, if no charity or charities is(are) named, the entire estate, including the three hundred fifty million dollars cash awarded you in Item 1, reverts to a holding trust, to be distributed in the form of low-interest small business loans. This is your final challenge. It is within your power to determine now the futures of countless possible recipients.

"Finally, Item 3: I reveal to you now the significance of the red satin ribbon which secured the original rolled vellum document found within the radio. Take the ribbon to Raventon General Hospital and give it to Taylor's doctor. Tell him to tie the ribbon around Taylor's left wrist."

With that, the man slipped the document back into its envelope.

"You have thirty minutes from now to make your decisions regarding Item 2."

Pilfree looked at the wall clock above the cash register. It read eight-thirty+. He sighed and turned to Bobbie Leigh.

"We've won the lottery, Pilfree," Bobbie Leigh said.

"Yes, but how do we want the other part distributed?"

"*Other* part? Can't it go to *us*, too?"

"No, it *can't* go to us! Didn't you *listen?* And I hope you have that red satin ribbon."

"Hard to hear *anything* with ninety million dollars clogging your ears. I thought *you* had the ribbon."

"It's *not* ninety million! It's a *hundred sixteen* million. And some change," Pilfree said, looking again at the wall clock. "Let me check my backpack pockets for that ribbon. Check yours, too."

"*Whatever!*" Bobbie Leigh said, rifling through her backpack pockets. "Either amount will sure buy a lot of jeans and junk. Not in my backpack."

"Is that *all* you ... look, we've got twenty-five minutes to decide who gets Blythington's remaining estate, at least six hundred fifty million dollars. *Found* it! Hold this, and *don't* lose it."

"Hmmm," Bobbie Leigh said, taking the ribbon from Pilfree.

"The money has to advance the *human* condition, Bobbie Leigh, not *your* condition."

"Aren't I human, too?"

"Sometimes I wonder," Pilfree whispered.

"Advance the human condition, you say? How about bigger malls, or better yet, how about *better* malls, malls with bigger stores, more floors, no stupid music, and best of all ... wait for it ... *everyday is Black Friday!*"

Pilfree stared with incredulity at Bobbie Leigh. Retaining calm, he took a deep breath. "Bobbie Leigh," he said, "what do you think about maybe doing *something* to help out *Taylor's* condition, those who suffer terribly from conditions such as Taylor's?"

"Like what?"

Pilfree noted the time. 8:47.

"Think *cures*," he said, hoping the idea would spring into Bobbie Leigh's mind, thus making his idea mutual.

"Cures? As in *manicures?*"

"Try again."

Bobbie Leigh closed her eyes and thought hard, though somehow eluding the obvious. 8:54. She pulled the red satin ribbon between her fingers. Then, struck by an epiphany, a smile stretched across her face.

"Cancer cures!" she shouted.

"*Yes*, Bobbie Leigh! Brilliant! Now help me decide who gets the money to fund cancer research. I know it's asking a lot, but we haven't much time and *you're* going to have to think fast."

"Ha, ha, very funny," Bobbie Leigh said. "Okay, here it is. Three hundred million goes to Raventon General Hospital to fund their new cancer research center."

"Check," Pilfree confirmed.

"The rest, the remaining three hundred million dollars, goes to—"

"You mean three hundred *fifty* million.

"*Whatever!* Who can do the math with such large numbers! The rest goes to St. Jude Children's ... something something," Bobbie Leigh declared.

"St. Jude Children's Research Hospital, you mean?"

"*That!* Yes!"

Pilfree looked at the wall clock. 8:59.

"Those are our choices, sir."

"So be it," the man said, jotting notes onto a pad of paper. "And well done. You will receive your reward via electronic funds transfer into accounts established in your names at First National Bank of Raventon. Expect your deposits no later than Monday end-of-day. I bid you good day."

The man stood and exited through the drape he'd entered from.

"*Wait!*" shouted Pilfree.

"He's gone, Pilfree."

Pilfree sighed. "Let's call Taylor's mom."

"Why don't we just walk over to the hospital, talk to her there and bring her doctor this ribbon?"

"Good idea. I wonder what purpose the ribbon serves, anyway?"

"Who knows?" Bobbie Leigh said, shrugging. "It's by far the easiest part of the challenges."

"So, hold tight to it."

"Count on it." Bobbie Leigh looked toward the clock tower's top, dawn's sun rays illuminating its snow-white paint. "Can all this have been *real*, Pilfree? I mean, a hundred and sixteen million each? *Really?*"

"Seemed real. My *thumb* believes it was real," he said, lifting his left hand. "I guess we'll know for sure next Monday."

"I guess." Bobbie Leigh paused. "Wait'll Taylor learns of her fortune."

"I suspect the only fortune she cares about is her health, her life. I know that's all *I* care about."

"Same here."

They walked on, silent.

"Think it'll be enough? The money, that is," Bobbie Leigh asked. "To help Taylor?"

"Let's hope," Pilfree said, reaching into his backpack. "She can always have my share."

"Mine, too."

"Oh, good."

"What now, Pil-boy?"

"I know *this* is real." He lifted his hand. "Poptart." Pilfree offered it to Bobbie Leigh. She took it, breaking it in half, returning the gesture.

Meanwhile, Taylor rested in her hospital room, eyes closed and wearing the smile of omniscience, as she awaited her friends, her teammates.

Mike held her hand, returning her smile, as he straightened the drawstrings of his black hoodie.

"What's life all about, anyway, Dad?"

"About? Oh, I don't know, Taylor," Mike answered. "Maybe life's all about living."

"And loving?"

"And loving, too, sweetheart. It's no more of a game than that, I suppose."

"Uncle Blythington was quite a man, wasn't he?" Taylor whispered.

"Quite a man."

www.ingramcontent.com/pod-product-compliance
Lightning Source LLC
Chambersburg PA
CBHW031614240626
47153CB00002B/752

* 9 7 8 0 9 8 1 4 7 4 8 7 8 *